A FALL FROM GRACE

When Detective Charlie Peace attains the rank of inspector he decides to relocate his family to the sleepy town of Slepton Edge. Soon after arriving, Charlie and his wife Felicity encounter a group of children chanting outside a home, but the residents, a retired elderly couple who have recently moved in, cannot explain the children's actions. Strangely, the children seem well organised and some of their chants are lines from Shakespeare's *The Tempest*. When a mysterious death disturbs the community, the network of neighbourhood gossip emerges as both Charlie's greatest ally and the biggest obstacle in his path to the truth.

A FALL FROM GRACE

A FALL FROM GRACE

by

Robert Barnard

Magna Large Print Books
Long Preston, North Yorkshire,
BD23 4ND, England.

British Library Cataloguing in Publication Data.

Barnard, Robert
    A fall from grace.

    A catalogue record of this book is
    available from the British Library

    ISBN   978-0-7505-2632-6

First published in Great Britain 2007 by Allison & Busby Ltd.

Copyright © 2007 by Robert Barnard

Cover illustration © Old Tin Dog Design

The moral right of the author has been asserted

Published in Large Print 2007 by arrangement with
Allison & Busby Ltd.

Magna Large Print is an imprint of Library Magna Books Ltd.

Printed and bound in Great Britain by
T.J. (International) Ltd., Cornwall, PL28 8RW

1

Prospecting

Charlie Peace came out of the door of Blackett and Podmore the estate agents holding a sheaf of property descriptions. He slipped into his car, parked on the edge of the little square in the centre of the village, and began to riffle through them.

Ten minutes later he got on the mobile to his wife.

'Well, there seem to be several houses here that might suit, going by the descriptions.'

'You can't,' said Felicity.

'I know. There are lies, damned lies and estate agents' brochures,' he said. 'Trouble is, you only get to plumb the depths of their deceptions when you've actually lived in the places they've sold for a few months.'

'And it doesn't help that we're looking for two places rather than just one.'

Driving off on a circuit of inspections of exteriors mapped out for him by the maligned estate agents, Charlie echoed Felicity's words. His attaining the rank of inspector some months earlier had coincided with a proposal from his father-in-law who, on the first hint that the new job might enable Charlie and Felicity to move out of Leeds, had decided that he needed to move in with or close to them.

'Close to,' Charlie had said firmly. 'Not in with.'

'Not on your life,' Felicity had agreed. 'I'm not going to be his dogsbody.'

She knew her father through and through, of course. Rupert Coggenhoe had used people (notably his wife) throughout his life, and Felicity knew that old age would not have changed him, though she felt twinges of guilt at the thought that the only thing that would change him was by now fairly close. He had made a respectable living writing novels in a variety of genres, effortlessly shifting styles without ever becoming a complete master in any one of them. He had explained to his daughter and son-in-law that his cottage – a kind of super-cottage, with various extensions at the back, to which he had moved from Luton when he had come into a windfall legacy from a great-aunt – would fetch around four hundred thousand pounds, a tribute to the enduring appeal of the West Country. He proposed to part-finance his daughter and son-in-law's purchase of a house for their growing family. The only catch was that the house had to have a granny-flat, or to be near some other, smaller property which he would purchase for himself.

'To which you will be called to cook, clean, garden and hold his awful old hand,' said Charlie, not scared of seeming ungrateful when in his opinion so little gratitude was called for.

'Just not possible,' said Felicity complacently. 'I won't be able to leave Carola and little Foetus.'

Little Foetus was growing, but they had not tried to learn his sex, so had not given it a proper name.

'Could be Evelyn,' said Felicity. 'Or Hilary or Lesley. Do for either sex.'

'Evelyn Peace,' said Charlie, turning up his nose. 'Sounds like a writer of soppy verse.'

The tour around Slepton Edge, which he'd thought of as a typical small village but which probably housed about two thousand inhabitants, took nearly half an hour. He discarded the few properties with granny flats, not because they were too small, though they were, but because he didn't want his father-in-law so near. Then he started sifting through the rest, noting down the properties he would like to live in that had another small property fairly near that was also for sale. His father-in-law's property in Devon was of the sort that had roses and hollyhocks peeping through its earholes, arsehole and all intermediate orifices. Charlie had taken an instant dislike to it the

9

one time he visited it, at the time of his mother-in-law's funeral. He thought a farm-hand's two-up, two-down was not going to be suitable for the old fraud in a few years' time, so he preferred to set his sights on a modern bungalow, with or without roses and hollyhocks. It was a sensible and achievable objective, and he drove back to the centre of the village with three pairs of properties he wanted to view the insides of.

He came out of Blackett and Podmore's with all the arrangements having been made: he and Felicity would view all the bungalows the next evening, since it was obviously useless to see any property on his own, especially as he was not prepared to shoulder sole responsibility if the choice proved a disaster. Felicity's more (but not particularly) domestic eye was needed to adjudicate on the pluses and minuses of all the prospective dwellings. Vital that she have her say before and not after the decision. Something was going on in the centre of Slepton Edge as he drove back into town. He had noticed a long, gangling, youngish man with a shy but eager smile busying himself there when he'd first been to the agents'. Now the young man had taken over the little central area of the square, where a monument to the Marquis of Wakefield, a local benefactor, was sited. A tiny stage – hardly more than a soapbox – had been erected in front of the statue, and a microphone, with wires leading to a generator, was attached to its front. The gangling man was testing it as Charlie watched, helped by a pregnant woman of about his own age – early thirties, Charlie estimated – and by a little group of supporters.

Perhaps more surprising, a knot of listeners was already clustering on the pavements on either side of the square – smiling, greeting each other, waiting for things to start. It was very unlike an election. In any case there was no General Election going on, and so far as Charlie knew no by-election either: the police were always on the alert during a by-election, but particularly since so many of the northern ones had a candidate fielded by the British National Party with rabidly racist programmes and literature. His musings were interrupted by the man's first words booming into the crowd.

'You all know there's an election on. For the first time people in this area can vote as to who should become mayor of Halifax. And I think most of you know that I'm a candidate.'

There was applause – more than polite, in fact decidedly warm. Charlie had got over his surprise. Elections for mayor, on the American model, had been on the cards for three or four years now, depending on the choice of the area. Presumably the people – or perhaps the bigwigs – of Halifax, in which Slepton Edge was situated, had decided to try having an elected mayor. As a rule the mayor was at best a useful local representative of many years standing in local government, or at worst a party hack due for an empty honour as his reward before retirement. The good voters of Halifax or their elected representatives must have decided to go for something a bit more colourful and out-of-the-ordinary.

'You know who I am, but the people around us, in Halifax for example, won't know. And I won't be able to say "I'm your Labour candidate" or "Your Conservative candidate". That's very useful, that is: it's like saying "Don't vote for me, vote for my label". We've been doing that for too long. If you vote for me you'll be voting for a person, not a label. Who am I? Well, I'm a doctor, and that's what you'll be voting for, even though I'm not practising at the moment. I was for five years a consultant in ear, nose and throat complaints at a big hospital. Before that I'd been in general practice. Then I gave it all up. I thought I was taking a holiday, but in fact I was sign- ing up for a new way of life. I was tired of what was happening in the Health Service.'

There was a smattering of applause at this, and 'So are we all' came from one man.

'It wasn't a matter of money. That's part of the problem, but only a part. I was fed up with quick fixes. Is there a waiting list? Lower the average time a patient has with his specialist to five minutes. Slice one category of patients off the list. If these don't work, just fiddle the figures. Is the drug bill too high? Notice they say "drugs", not "medicines". Drugs sounds vaguely nasty, something we should avoid. All right, stop doctors prescribing the new, expensive drugs. Say certain conditions shouldn't be treated at all. Charge the patient market prices for his care. I got out because we don't have a Health Service any more. We have a confidence trick based on the quick fix and the clever fiddle.'

Charlie was by now out of his car and listening intently. The crowd had grown, was genial, supportive, and whenever the man made a friendly move towards them they reciprocated. He was not an orator. Charlie had often marvelled that men like Hitler and Mussolini, mediocre of mind and unprepossessing of body, could by means of that black art which is mass oratory be transformed into vehicles of destruction. But this man just talked to his audience – no ego trip, no mesmerism. Yet in ten minutes he had them in the palms of his hands. They admired him. In a way they seemed to love him. What a wonderful thing! And what a dangerous one!

'Think!' the man went on, clearly drawing to a conclusion. 'We've had real, independent men in our parliament since the last two elections. We need more. And we need many, many more in local government. That shouldn't be a party thing at all. We want men who consider issues, think them through, and when they've come to a conclusion work to bring about a better state of affairs. We want men who are their own men, and women who are their own women. Vote for me!'

All this was done with half a smile on his face, perhaps to show that he was serious but not too serious. When he finished there was a respectably enthusiastic cheer and a lot of applause. He got down from his improvised platform and started mingling with the small crowd. Charlie watched him curiously. It became clear that he knew almost all of them. He heard him greeting people by their Christian names. A genuinely local man, then, he guessed. And other locals were willing to stand in the chill October sunshine to listen to him, then linger around to talk to him.

Charlie got back into his car and put his key in the ignition. Then, on an impulse, he changed his mind. He waited – watching the people disappear to homes, shops and pubs. The man went back to the pregnant woman still beside the platform, and together, with help from the two assistants, they began to pack up the sound equipment. Charlie waited until they were finished, then got out of the car and went over to them. The man

14

saw him, and smiled a candidate's smile of greeting.

'I thought electioneering speeches were a thing of the past,' Charlie said.

'So were independent candidates,' said the man. 'But they're making a modest comeback, and I'm trying to give an extra shove. I'm Chris Carlson, by the way.'

Charlie's glance went to the election poster on a stick which had been turned away from his car when the man was speaking.

'Or Dr Chris Carlson,' Charlie said. The man shrugged good-humouredly.

'Once a doctor, always a doctor,' he said.

'Why throw away a good selling point?' said the woman beside him. 'I'm Alison Carlson. The wife.'

'I'm Charlie Peace.'

'And are you thinking of coming to live here?' asked Dr Carlson. 'I saw you coming out of the estate agents'.'

'Maybe. This is one of the places we're looking at. But I don't expect we'll be in time to vote for you.'

'Never mind. That wasn't why I asked. I'm serious about standing for mayor, but I'm not desperate to get elected. How about a cup of tea and a muffin? Alison has to get home and rest, and I'm always interested in a new face.'

'Sure,' said Charlie, with that feeling familiar to policemen of being glad to be wanted.

They raised their hands to Alison and the other two helpers storing the equipment away in an old car, then crossed the road towards a tea-room called the Hot Muffin.

'Only started up three months ago,' said Dr Chris. 'I think she's struggling a bit. Hello Hilda, this is – sorry, I've forgotten your name.'

'Charlie Peace.'

'He's thinking of moving here.' She showed them to a table, and they began poring over their menus. 'Moving here with wife? With kids perhaps?'

'Yes, both. One little girl and another unspecified on the way.'

'And you want to move out of the city? Yes, I thought so. We've got one on the way too, as you'll have noticed. It's like a reward, or maybe a benediction. I say, we could betroth the two at birth, like in a Dickens novel – if they turn out to be of different sex, of course.'

'Sounds like a recipe for disaster,' said Charlie. 'Anyway, if our Carola is anything to go by it wouldn't work. She decides everything – and I mean *every*thing – for herself. She might consider a suggestion, but she'd never accept dictation... Why did you say your sprog would be a reward or a benediction?'

Dr Chris turned to Hilda, and ordered tea and hot muffins.

16

'Benediction for giving up the practice of medicine. People sometimes suggest it was irresponsible or worse. But the sprog is like someone is saying "You did the right thing". Actually, what it really means, I suppose, is that we both became more relaxed, certainly more happy, and simply had more time. Giving up work – that work – has been like a liberation. It's as if I was a new person, and that applies to Alison too. The fact that I've slipped my fetters means an entirely new sort of life for her.'

'You're never going back?'

He shrugged, suggesting genuine uncertainty.

'Not so far as I know – certainly not in the immediate future.'

'What do you do with your time?'

'What time?... No, I'm joking, but it all does seem to get filled. I do all sorts of things. Mostly I paint. I hadn't had a paintbrush in my hand for years – not since my first long vacation from medical school. But I've always loved it. I'm not *good*, don't think that. But I'm a good amateur, and my landscapes strike a chord in your average art-fancier who knows what he likes.'

'So you make a living out of it?'

'I'm just starting to. I take them round the classy shopping malls, have little exhibitions in Harrogate, Ilkley, places like that. We'll not starve when the little one comes.'

17

'With a nice lot stashed away from your time as consultant,' said Charlie dryly. Chris laughed.

'My complaint was never about the pay. What's wrong with the health service is the deal that patients are getting.'

'And everyone here knows you're a doctor, I notice.'

'Oh yes.'

'And they come to you with their little ailments and worries?'

'How did you know?'

'I'm a policeman. We're experts at spotting the obvious. No, that's not true. In fact we have to really struggle to know what ordinary people do, because we usually see people who are at the worst end of "ordinary". But I could see you were sympathetic and approachable with the crowd outside. Of course they'd bring you their troubles.'

'I squared it with the local group of GPs,' said Chris, as if he needed to apologise. 'It takes from their shoulders a lot of visits from people who just want to talk things over, want to be reassured that their little pains in the area of the heart, their twinges in the back, are not signals to give up the struggle for living. And I sometimes alert them to something that might be serious, and make the sufferer go along to see them. If I say they need to get something checked up, they generally go.'

18

'I'm sure they do. You're persuasive.'

'And what about you? Are you a persuasive policeman?'

Charlie laughed. It wasn't a question he'd ever been asked.

'I'm not sure persuasion is a weapon we use very much. Mild bullying, tricking, threatening... Oh, I do a job of work that is much less salubrious than yours.'

'Still, I expect people here would be quite pleased to have another policeman living among them.'

'Maybe. I hope I can be an off-duty one. I haven't actually spoken to anyone yet apart from you. Felicity and I are viewing some places tomorrow night.'

'Remember people here are a little conservative. Don't be too harsh on them.'

Charlie understood at once what he meant.

'Believe me, I know all the range of facial expressions of people who open their doors to a black face: everything from shock-horror to pleased anticipation. I've learnt not to pay too much attention to initial reactions over the years.'

'Forgive me. Of course you have. I don't suppose there's anything I could teach you about black-white relations.'

Charlie's face showed amusement rather than anger.

'Felicity is white, by the way. That helps. You might think it would be the reverse, but

I think the white person provides a sort of way into the situation for the kind of person who lives in a place like Slepton. We shall bring my father-in-law with us if we come here, though I'm not sure he'd be much use in a sticky racial situation.'

'So you've got three generations living together. That's good of you.'

'*Not* living together, and not good of us at all. He's going to buy a separate house, and he's helping us with our mortgage. Don't sentimentalise us, and don't sentimentalise him. My father-in-law is a selfish, clinging, narcissistic and emotionally blood-sucking apology for a father.' He looked around the sparsely-patronised tea-rooms. 'One of the appeals of this place may turn out to be the predominantly elderly population, which will give him a circle to drop into. The fact that he's a writer will help that.'

'Oh really? What does he write?'

'Everything. Anything he thinks will sell. He's also bitterly resentful that he's never had a bestseller. Among his pseudonyms are Jed Parker and Chantalle Derivaux, which gives you an idea of his range. If we can get some people reading his books, and if they will tell him how much they enjoyed them, which they usually do with authors, then things may go swimmingly. Disraeli should have said "Everyone enjoys flattery, and when it comes to authors you should lay it on with a trowel".' Charlie got up. 'It's time I was making a move.'

'Must you go? I'm enjoying this conversation.'

'And I'm on duty. I'll have to disguise this break by pretending I was investigating whether there is a British National Party presence at this election.'

'There isn't. They probably don't think the job of mayor is one of sufficient power to justify their muscling in on it. And of course in this country it isn't.'

'Why are you standing then?'

'Shall we say for a bit of fun? Though that's only part of the truth. I do feel that the party system has stifled genuine debate, polarised opinions in a totally unhelpful way, and led to the sort of yah-boo politics that gets us nowhere. It *is* time for a change. We need a solid block of true independents who look at every issue in a clear-eyed way.'

'Well, I'll wish you good luck,' said Charlie, shaking his hand. 'And I really will be following your progress with interest.'

In the event that turned out to be more easily said than done. When he got home he found that his father-in-law had dumped himself on them, having sold his cottage, hollyhocks and all, to a buyer who wanted to move in immediately. He became cagey when he was asked why he hadn't even given them a phone call to warn them. Clearly he had

21

feared excuses, lodgings found for him, obdurate refusals of hospitality. So speed was now of the essence. The next evening Charlie and Felicity viewed the three properties in Slepton Edge, along with the smaller ones, and chose two. The one they chose for themselves was a stone house dating from the 1880s with three rooms downstairs and four bedrooms upstairs, one of them marked down as a study for Felicity who followed the parental example in one thing only: the urge to write fiction. There was a little scrap of garden at the front and a larger one at the back, clearly destined to be a playing area for two, which Charlie decided on the spot would be nothing but grass. Mowing he could enjoy; planting, tending, weeding and pruning he didn't have time for, and wouldn't until he reached retirement age.

The bungalow they chose for Rupert Coggenhoe was five minutes away, gently uphill and on the edge of the inhabited part of the village, with nature, metaphorically speaking, on its doorstep. Felicity's dad had said that he relied entirely on their judgment, which gave him unlimited opportunities for whingeing once he had moved in.

The choice having been made, it was time for the lawyers, surveyors, solicitors and removalists to take over, and on Charlie and Felicity's part a constant and successful effort to get the transaction finalised and the move made as soon as possible. At work, reading the Yorkshire papers during a quiet spell, Charlie learnt that the election for mayor of Halifax had been won by the Labour candidate Archie Skelton, a party stalwart in his sixties, but that Dr Christopher Carlson had come a respectable and surprising second, having been beaten by only 267 votes.

And that was the situation when, on the thirteenth of November, Charlie and Felicity, accompanied by Carola and the foetus, moved to 15 Walsh Street, Slepton Edge. Mr Rupert Coggenhoe, accompanied only by his half-finished manuscript novel *Georgia Cavendish*, came with them in the car and had his first sight of his Fifties bungalow, 23 Forsythia Avenue, Slepton Edge. From Charlie and Felicity's point of view it was near enough for help to be on hand, but not quite far enough for comfort. As for Coggenhoe, he sighed, as if it wasn't really his sort of place at all and they should have known that, but allowed himself to be led out of the car and shown around.

2

Settling In

The process of the Peace family getting themselves settled in to the new house in Slepton Edge took three days, days which Charlie took off from work, to toil but also to enjoy. They took Carola with them on those days but not Felicity's father, counting on Carola as being less trouble. Not only was she that, but she was also an excellent talking point with neighbours, shopkeepers and people met casually in streets and in pubs. On the fourth day Charlie returned to work in Leeds and Felicity supervised her father's move from Leeds to Slepton.

In itself it went perfectly well. All the furniture which had been in storage since her father had moved from the hollyhocked cottage arrived on the morning of the move, fitted well into the new bungalow, and by evening all was so settled and convenient that he was able to sleep the night in his own bed in his own house. Whether that was what he wanted was another matter. He claimed that he had not eaten since they had left him alone in Leeds, and when Felicity pointed out that there were plenty of good cafés, restaurants and pubs nearby, he sighed and said he couldn't splash out money intended for them when he was Gone (the capital letter was his). He also said that things in Slepton (of which he had seen almost nothing) were Not What He Was Used To, but at least, he said, he would be near to them.

That, Felicity thought, was not a comfort but the principal fly in the ointment.

Still, the situation admitted of several hopeful factors. On the trips she and Rupert took around Slepton to introduce him to shopkeepers, pub landlords and café proprietors several people recognised them and stopped. 'You must be the author,' some said. Or, even better: 'You must be Rupert Coggenhoe, the author. I've read several of your books.'

Chris Carlson had been doing a propaganda job. They had been at his house a couple of times in the middle of the moving process, and had liked both him and his wife. They had told him more about Felicity's father, and the problems and dangers he presented, and he had obviously taken measures in his usual quiet but efficient way.

This recognition of her father, however artificially induced, seemed after a few days to be paying off. The arrival of Coggenhoe, the author, was generating in sleepy Slepton the sort of interest that in such places passes for excitement. Slepton Edge had a great many retired people among its inhabitants, as well as some like Dr Carlson who were re-designing their lives. New stimuli, new topics of conversation, were just what was needed in such an environment, and during his first weeks in the village Rupert Coggenhoe enjoyed something very close to popularity. Most of his new readers were women, but there was the odd male one too, and by being sociable in the tea-room and in one or other of the two pubs, he gathered around himself something that could be called a circle.

'Things are going much better than I thought they would,' said Charlie, when they went into the Black Heifer one night a few days later after leaving Carola in the children's play area and saw Rupert already surrounded by an admiring group near the bar.

'He's even doing some of his own shopping,' agreed Felicity. 'So as to meet his admirers. Let's just hope it lasts.'

Their own company that evening was a recent new acquaintance, Desmond Pinkhurst, who ambled over to their table, looking around the large bar apparently in quest of someone, before sinking disappointed into a chair beside Felicity. Desmond had been a mildly celebrated young actor forty years before, best known for his 'silly ass' roles in British comedy films, as well as occasional similar roles in sitcoms and British musicals, at a time when they were mainly Noel-Coward-and-water. Now, after twenty years of retirement on a share portfolio that was the greatest emotional interest in his life, he was – on the surface – bumbling, well-intentioned, accident-prone and in love with his own anxieties.

'I wondered if...' he began, his eyes still going everywhere, '...but never mind. How *are* you both? And how is your distinguished father, my dear?'

'We are fine. We are settled in, we no longer trip over the furniture because it's in different places, and we're enjoying Slepton and its people,' said Charlie.

'And as to my father, I think most of that applies to him too. It's a big wrench, at his age, moving, uprooting himself. But he's survived, and he's been made very welcome.'

'So I see,' said Desmond. 'All the fairer sex fluttering around him.'

'Are you jealous?' asked Felicity. 'Or perhaps grateful to him for getting them off your back?'

'I see you've been listening to local gossip,' said Desmond, archly.

'Gossip?'

Desmond leaned forward, in confiding mode.

'To the effect that I'm gay. Don't you believe it. I'm not gay at all. Just not particularly heterosexual.'

He looked round triumphantly, as if that

explained everything.

'I see,' said Felicity.

'In places like this they say that about anyone who hasn't been married,' Desmond went on. 'And I sometimes have male friends from the profession staying with me, and some of them *are* gay.'

'But you're not?'

'Oh dear no! Just not all that *in*terested, as I say.'

He grinned at them both. Charlie had the sense of having old jokes and old obfuscations tried out on him, as a newcomer. He noticed that as the man sent his grin around the table the questing glance went too.

'Are you waiting for someone?' Charlie asked him. Desmond nodded.

'Oh, just for Chris. I want to ask his advice. It's rather a shock, and I don't quite know...'

'What's rather a shock?'

Desmond settled hunched over the table.

'Well, I've just had the offer of a job. A stage job. It's years since that happened. And the poor old stock portfolio has been down a bit these last few months, and so – well, I'm tempted. It's not as if I'm *in need*, but still...'

'So what's the problem?'

'It's in Sheffield. Too far to drive to rehearsals and performances. Much too far for me. Even Halifax is an adventure. I shouldn't be allowed on the road. And then, it's such a strange thing to offer me. I mean, *Ibsen*. I've hardly ever done anything really serious, let alone something so ... you know ... intellectually challenging – that's really what I mean. And there's already talk of a transfer to London.'

So there it was. The Great Norwegian, intimidating as usual, his British reputation for unrelieved doom and gloom sending shivers down Desmond Pinkhurst's spine for fear he should spoil things by letting cheerfulness break in. Charlie, who was very much a get-up-and-do-it sort of person, played down the Ibsen side and concentrated on the joy and stimulus of working again, of performing before an audience. Desmond remained congenitally uncertain.

'I don't know, really I don't... There is pathos in the character, and some humour. It's Old Ekdal in *The Wild Duck*. It's not often been done in recent years because there's a fairly large cast – lots of small parts. They prefer the later plays with a tiny cast. It's all money these days, isn't it?'

'But the money would come in handy, I suppose?' Charlie asked.

'Oh, it *would*. But learning the part, and the nerves – I'm a bag of nerves, particularly with stage roles. I was always a film and television man.' He thought. 'I once had a small part in *Coronation Street*. One of Rita Fairclough's boyfriends. But of course that's a quite different matter from Ibsen. Ibsen!

The very thought makes me shiver! I really don't know... Oh, there he is.'

And there Chris was. He was buying himself a pint of bitter and swapping greetings with Sid the landlord, but already positioned by his right arm was a stout elderly lady, her eyes on his face, waiting for any sign of an end to the conversation, when she would wade in to get reassurance about a twinge or an ache or a tic. The expression on her face spoke of something close to adoration. And behind the two of them, now, was Desmond, who had got across the expanse of the saloon bar in a surprisingly nippy manner, glass in hand, and was now waiting his turn. Charlie looked at Felicity.

'I don't know how Chris does it,' he said. 'Advice to an old dear on cutting down on the chocolates, and to an old Thespian on whether or not to take a part in a play.'

Felicity looked at Chris with the assessing eye of someone who herself wrote (as yet unpublished) novels, and liked things she could make use of.

'He is so immensely likeable,' she said. 'I suppose people find that they can just talk away to him and he understands, and just by the process of talking they sort things out in their minds in a way that solitary thinking, and having all the options crowding in on you without any sorting or classifying, doesn't do.'

'I expect you're right,' said Charlie. 'Though I'm not sure I would want that sort of responsibility myself.'

'Responsibility? How does he have responsibility?'

'Because even if all he does, most of the time, is listen, they'll associate him in their minds with whatever decision they take.'

'They could, I suppose,' said Felicity thoughtfully. 'Especially if they're not logical thinkers.'

'Do you see poor old Desmond as a clear-minded thinker? Oh hell – watch it. Here comes our own personal problem figure.'

It was Felicity's father, steaming over with a female in tow. Charlie and Felicity had agreed when speculating on Rupert's future that he would try to find a substitute for his dead wife. This would not be, or not primarily, to perform her conjugal duties, but to do the other things, including household chores, laundry, shopping and cooking, above all ego-boosting. Felicity had already observed him returning to his bungalow with a variety of women after morning coffee, pub lunches, or weekly shopping. When he now introduced Nancy Stoppard, Felicity remembered that she had already been mentioned by Chris Carlson as 'a pleasant widow with a bit of money'. Jackpot!

'Nancy, this is my daughter whom you've heard me mention. Felicity, and her husband who everyone calls Charlie for no good reason that I can see, and outside playing on the slide is little Carola, the light of my life, my only grandchild until the little one there decides to make his entrance into this wicked world.'

Coggenhoe had a unique ability to make everything he said grate on his daughter. It had been explained to him many times why Dexter Peace had popularly become Charlie (and it didn't need a mastermind to work it out), and he had in fact paid remarkably little attention to his granddaughter Carola since he came north, partly because she was too young to be useful to him, and perhaps partly because she was a child with a strong will of her own. Not the sort of female that Rupert tried to attract.

'Nice to meet you,' said Nancy, shaking hands. 'Rupert has talked so much about you.'

As she said this Charlie saw an expression waft quickly across her face as she realised that her wholly conventional words were not in this case true: Rupert Coggenhoe had talked very little about his family.

'When is the baby due?' she asked, sticking to convention.

'May,' said Felicity. 'Carola's was a fairly easy birth, and I'm hoping this will be the same.'

'But until then *we* have to take good care

of *her*, instead of her taking good care of us,' said her father. Grate, grate.

'You have always taken *very* good care of yourself, Dad.'

'And she won't have much time to take care of anyone except herself and the babe for a long time after the birth,' said Nancy. 'Even Charlie and Carola will miss out.'

'I'm used to it,' said Charlie. 'Carola will create blue murder.'

'Then you must stop spoiling her from now on,' said Nancy. 'Restrict all your care to talking, sympathising and advising.'

Felicity laughed.

'We've just been talking about that. I don't think there's any need in Slepton Edge for that sort of service.'

'Yes, we do have our regular shoulder to cry on,' said Nancy, looking to the other end of the bar, where Desmond had got his place in the sun and was talking earnestly to Chris. His hands sometimes made actorish gestures, but from him they seemed deeply, anguishedly in earnest.

'Desmond's been offered a stage part,' said Charlie. 'In *The Wild Duck*. He's not sure he's up to it, not sure he wants the bother. But I think the money would come in useful.'

'He should take it,' said Felicity. 'It's a lovely part – funny, but tender and pathetic as well.'

'I hear that he's never done anything

except Silly-Billy parts,' said Rupert, nakedly contemptuous of his rival celebrity. 'Not much of a preparation for Ibsen.'

'I'm not so sure,' said Nancy. 'You sometimes get these comedians and soap stars who suddenly get a chance of a really meaty role and they make a wonderful success of it. He could be at the start of a whole new career. He should go for it.'

She looked studiously away from Rupert Coggenhoe's sneering face. Charlie thought she was an intelligent woman, if only because she agreed with him. If he was right she would not last long as Coggenhoe's favoured aide and helpmeet. He leaned forward and picked up glasses.

'Same again, everyone, or a change of tipple?'

At the bar he found himself next to Chris Carlson.

'How's the surgery going?' he asked.

'Quite well,' said Chris, a tiny wafting of irritation crossing his face. 'But you're being mischievous as usual. You know I don't do medical advice. The most I do is pass them on to someone who will, if I think there's anything that needs checking over.'

'I'm sure you act impeccably, and I'm sure you save the local GPs from a lot of fruitless surgery sessions. But I meant a sort of emotional surgery. Advice for the sorely tried and bewildered.'

'Ah, poor old Desmond,' said Chris sagely. 'Well, I just let him talk the thing through. I can't advise him, but I can listen. I think underneath he desperately wants to experience again the excitement of being on stage, and all the backstage gossip and bitchery.'

'I expect you're right, though the fear at the top isn't going to go away, and it will be worse at his age. But I'm sure you help them to think things through for themselves.'

'I try to. But you have your doubts, don't you?'

'Do I? I suppose my face is easily read... I'm not sure I can put the doubts into words. There seems to me a danger of you becoming necessary to people here – someone who is there when anything of any importance has to be discussed.'

'That makes me sound a frightful prig. But talking things through never did anyone any harm, did it? Why is there any danger in people doing that?'

'I really meant danger to you. Seeing yourself as a sort of moral arbiter to the whole village. You might start to see yourself as indispensable, whereas really you're just the icing on the cake. Now I sound a prig, don't I? But as a rule I find people only take advice that coincides with what they intend to do anyway.'

'Cynic. You make me feel quite useless. Oh, there's Alison. Over here, darling.'

By the time that she had pushed her pregnant way through the crowded bar Chris had been commandeered by a worried and bespectacled middle-aged man who Charlie classified in his mind as a schoolteacher. Charlie raised his eyebrows at Alison, added a Britvic Orange to his order, then shared the carrying with her so as to bring her over to his table. He did this with intent, and it worked like a dream: when his father-in-law saw the approach of another pregnant woman he began to show signs of unease, and when Charlie said he'd go out and fetch Carola in as it was getting too cold for her to be outside, he heard as he was retreating the sound of Rupert and Nancy's chairs scraping and excuses being made.

Carola was being looked after by a mother with her own small son, and she was reluctant to come in. By the time he had carried her through the bar the two pregnant women were finished with signs and symptoms and were on to Alison's evening.

'It was the Townswomen's Guild, at Halifax,' she was saying. 'Quite a good lecture. I was someone's guest – I promised to go during the election. But when I got there I found there was nobody else there under the age of fifty-five.'

'Why on earth did you go?' Felicity asked. 'The election is over. You don't need anyone's vote.'

'Oh, I'd promised. Anyway, you never know. Chris says that Archie Skelton, the man who won, shows classic signs of heart problems.'

Charlie raised his eyebrows.

'Is this a case of ambulance chasing? Did he tell the poor man, or is he waiting for him to drop dead?'

'He told him, of course,' said Alison, aiming a mock-blow at his head. 'Told him after the count. It turned out he knew perfectly well, but he was determined to go ahead and stand for mayor. He said if he only had a little time in the job it would still be worth it. You're very cynical about Chris, Charlie.'

'Charlie's very cynical about everything except Carola,' said Felicity.

'What's cynical?' asked Carola.

'A bit nasty,' said Charlie. 'And I'm not really cynical about Chris, but such goodness and usefulness and wisdom seem to demand some kind of counter-swing. He's got to have a downside to him.'

'Of course he has,' said Alison. 'But you'll have to find it out for yourself. I'm not going to hand it to you on a plate. You're a detective, after all. Do I detect, by the way, that the great Rupert Coggenhoe is rather sceptical about children?'

'*Yes*,' said Felicity. 'Small children and babies, because they can't be made to be impressed by him, and because they take up a great deal of people's time and attention.'

'Time and attention that he feels is his sole right and due,' said Charlie.

'But I'm not going to be negative about him,' said his wife, safe in having been just that. 'Things have gone so much better than we expected. Everyone here has been so kind and welcoming to him – and to us too, of course. I thought Dad was going to be a constant drain on my energies, particularly emotional ones. But he's got his own crowd around him almost at once, and he seems to get on very well with them, and to be *accepted*. It's all going swimmingly.'

Charlie thought at the time that Felicity was being more than a little complacent, but he was involved in playing 'Pat-a-cake, pat-a-cake, baker's man' with Carola, and didn't think twice about it. Until, that is, the letter came from Devon next morning.

3

The Innocents

The cottage in which Rupert Coggenhoe had spent the last few years of his life and the first years of his widowhood was in Coombe Barton, in Devon, in the well-heeled south-west, so when a letter arrived at the Peaces' the next day postmarked Newton Abbot no alarm bells were rung. Coggenhoe, when he wished to communicate, had usually rung them, not written, having a writer's natural reluctance to put pen to paper when no financial return could be expected.

The envelope was a large one, and it was puffed out with something soft as well as with paper. When Felicity and Charlie remembered the closeness of Newton Abbot to Rupert's old home they looked at the address, but it was for them not for Coggenhoe, and it had been forwarded from their former post office in Headingley. They looked at each other quizzically, and then opened it. The soft part of the package turned out to be a pair of Y-front underpants and a short-sleeved vest. The paper part consisted of a letter on lined notepaper, which ran:

Dear Felicity and your husband whose name I can't remember,

I enclose items of laundry which got put into my own draws and not found until recently. I hope your father has not missed them we were not speaking much in the last days. What happened was sad, but I'm sure there was faults and misunderstandings on both sides when you get to his age you sometimes do things you wouldn't have thought of doing when in your prime. Forget and forgive is my motto which some others here might follow but usually do not. The new people are about to move into the cottage and seem very nice. I'm sure things will turn out well in Yorkshire with you to look after him. I knew when I met you you were capable people, and you'll need to be.

Yours sincerely,
Madge Easton (Mrs)

They looked at each other. Felicity fingered the two garments, which somehow looked pathetic as well as ridiculous.

'I thought vests like that went out with the collapse of the coal-mining industry,' said Charlie.

'*What* has gone on?' said Felicity urgently. 'We need to know.'

'I'd *like* to know,' conceded Charlie. He walked over to the window and looked at the wilderness of back garden. He had a grand vision of calling some gardening firm in, and having a beautiful expanse of lawn in a matter of hours. Somehow November didn't seem the time to have it done, though. He turned back to Felicity. 'Even if we knew what it was, that doesn't mean we could prevent it happening again. Your father is not wise, and he's not receptive to advice.'

'Especially not from people less than half his age,' said Felicity.

'He wouldn't take it from people twice his age,' said Charlie.

'I wish I could remember Madge Easton,' said Felicity, her face wrinkled with the effort. 'We were only there for the funeral, and we met so many people... She'd never have called me "capable" if she'd known me before I met you, would she?'

'We've changed each other,' said Charlie, with unusual modesty. 'And you were always perfectly capable when you were away from your family. Your parents did tend to unnerve you, I'd admit. The first question is what use will your new capability be to keep your father in line?'

'No, it is: in what ways did he step out of line in Coombe Barton? What has he been up to, Charlie?' She looked down at the vest and underpants in her hands. 'We should put these away in the airing cupboard, or else throw them away. We can't return them to Dad without all sorts of questions being asked on both sides.'

'He can't have missed them,' agreed Charlie. 'And he could hardly ask about them if he had. Using the village ladies to do his laundry for him!' By the time Felicity returned from getting rid of the underwear Charlie had had time to re-read the letter. 'Cunning old bugger!' he said. 'It's obvious there was no question of a quick sale of his cottage and the new owners needing to move in. That was a lie. He took flight.'

'From something or other,' agreed Felicity. 'He'd become so unpopular he needed to move.'

'How do we find out? Ring Mrs Easton?'

But somehow they shrank from that. Checking up on so close a relative seemed distasteful – it was mixing Charlie's professional life too nearly with his private one. It seemed an invasion of Rupert's privacy, as well as treating him like a child – always the first thing to avoid with an ageing person. If he wanted to tell them what happened, he should be allowed to do it in his own time.

The nearest Felicity came to asking her father any of the vital questions was a few days later when he and she were walking companionably towards the shops, with Carola under protest in a pushchair, and her father was being greeted by several middle-aged-to-elderly women in the course of their progress along the main street of Slepton Edge.

'You are getting a little group around you,' said Felicity.

'Everyone is very kind,' Rupert replied, rather primly.

'It's just like at Coombe Barton. I still remember all those ladies at Mum's funeral. All with names like Doreen and Rose and Madge and Doris. Such dated names they seemed to have! I'm afraid if I met them again I wouldn't know them – wouldn't be able to distinguish Madge from Doris.'

42

'I sometimes found it difficult,' said Rupert, a touch of sourness mixing with primness.

'I suppose you will keep in touch, will you? Ring them up now and then?'

'Good Lord, no. If I phoned one I'd have to phone the lot.' He saw the disapproval on his daughter's face. 'Perhaps I'll send a card at Christmas,' he added lamely.

Then he dived into Gregg's the bakers, and began choosing a selection of sticky buns and cakes. Felicity did not remember her father having a sweet tooth, so she concluded that the sugary treats would be fed to what she was beginning to call his new harem. There was no taking up the conversation again.

A day or two later her attention was distracted from that particular matter in hand. She was on her way home from Chris and Alison's with Charlie and Carola. Charlie had wanted to talk over a case with Chris: a woman whose son had Huntington's chorea, who was suspected of making an attempt on the boy's life. He wanted to discuss the matter with a friend rather than a police doctor: the nature of the disease, the likely length of life after it had shown itself, if he'd known or heard of any comparable cases, and what sort of sentence the killer had received.

'But I suspect it's one of those crimes where sentencing will be all over the place, because sympathy and principles are in conflict,' he said bleakly. Chris, in any case, in his brief time in general practice had never had or known of a case of that disease.

Charlie and Felicity were still talking over the rights and wrongs of the matter and concluding that a right solution simply did not exist, when their ten minute walk took them as always past an estate of new houses. The Hatton Homes estate started on an old road just above their own house in Walsh Street, but extended into two fields that had been sold to developers ten years before. The houses were built in a yellowish brick that was off-putting in its resemblance to vomit, and the design of the houses gave the impression that each room had been squeezed in at the minimum possible size, so that everyone must be living in each other's pockets. But as they passed the edge of the estate, they heard the sound of children singing. Children's singing should have something of the angelic in it, but this singing did not. They stopped, and it was some minutes before they could distinguish the words of what was a chant more than a song.

''Ban, 'Ban, nowhere man,
Put yourself in the garbage can.'

They looked at each other. The chant was repeated, then was varied with assorted jeers – the tone was unmistakable, but the words were unclear. Charlie thought he caught 'rubbish tip' and 'down the sewer'. Felicity said:

'I don't like this.'

'Nor do I.'

'Can't you do anything?'

'It's probably racial,' said Charlie. 'A black policeman off his own pitch is not the best person to intervene. I'll get on the phone when we get home. Using a mobile would amount to provocation.'

'We need to know who's being targeted. I'll go and see if I can get a house number.'

Charlie swallowed back an objection, and merely said: 'Stay well away, and look casual.' He turned and walked on slowly, Carola clutching his hand. He was relieved when Felicity caught up to them.

'All the streets have tree names,' she said. 'The street I went up curves, and is called Willow Crescent. The children seem to be outside a house ten up from the one I was standing by, which was number fifteen. So say around number thirty-five.'

'And the children?'

'Two older children – girls of about fourteen or fifteen. The others a boy of about twelve, then four or five girls of about the same age or younger.'

'Urchins?'

'Not so far as I could see. Clean and tidy, even well-dressed. I didn't stop long enough to price their trainers.'

'Good job you didn't. Did you get what they were shouting?'

'Not much more than we heard – that the poor bloody people in the house were human rubbish. But that chant–'

''Ban, 'Ban–'

'Yes. It's based on *The Tempest:* "Ban, Ban, Ca-Caliban, Has a new master – Get a new man."'

'You must explain it some time. I suppose the kids are doing it at school.'

'Even the girls didn't look old enough to be doing GCSEs. And hardly any Shakespeare is being done lower down in schools these days.'

'Odd,' said Charlie. 'No sign of the residents?'

'Not a whisker. But I was a fair way away. What could they do? Lying low till the kids went away is pretty much their only option.'

When they got back home and Felicity was persuading Carola to bed, Charlie got on to his best contact in the Halifax force – a man called Peter Harridance: conscientious, thorough, a bit slow and cautious for Charlie's taste, but reliable.

'What have you got?' Felicity asked, when order and quiet had descended on the small bedroom upstairs and she came back down to find Charlie just putting down the phone.

'Well – not quite what we thought. A white couple called Norton, late sixties, recently gave up their own small independent bakery in the south – Lewes, he thought. They wanted to be near a daughter who's a teacher in Bradford. They sold their house in Sussex for much more than they paid up here, and they were delighted and pleased to be in a house "where everything worked" they said. No trouble whatever until two or three weeks ago. Then suddenly children started gathering in the street outside the front of the house. Not children they recognised from the Hatton Estate. First there were shoutings and jeers, then chanting. Not surprisingly they were upset by the language and direction of the taunts. No one likes to be told they're sink people, human garbage, and so on.'

'And they called the police?'

'Three days ago. That sort of thing isn't a priority – no crime involved – and by the time a couple of PCs arrived the children had gone. Apparently they generally are gone by nine o'clock – bedtime, presumably.'

'What did the police advise?'

'That the Nortons try talking to the children, find out what's bugging them, why they've got it in for people they don't even know.'

'I can't see *that* doing much good,' said Felicity tartly.

'No, it's not that impressive. But what would you advise?'

Felicity thought. Charlie often did this when she criticised police tactics.

'I admit I can't think of much. The same

thing but done by a policeman, I suppose: old people would probably appear dim bunglers to these kids, whereas the police would be no-nonsense and know what they were doing.'

'Touching. But bring in the police and that would be giving the matter a sort of importance it hardly deserves – priority over burglary, drunken violence, domestics – could you justify that?'

And Felicity had to admit that she couldn't.

It was two days later, when Charlie was just back from Leeds and changing out of his working clothes in the bedroom upstairs, that he saw the pack of children again. They must be the same children. They corresponded to Felicity's description: tidy, well-dressed and scrubbed: not a mob of cheerful urchins, but something more menacing. They were going past the house, very visible in the street lights, not talking or giggling together as might be expected, but walking slightly apart, and silently, as if on a secret mission or a raid – which probably was how it had been presented to the younger children, to add further spice and excitement. As they passed the house each of them, as if at some invisible sign, took out masks – rubber masks from pockets, hand-held masks from under jerseys and jackets. Then they turned, still silent, into the Hatton Homes estate and soon passed from view.

Charlie ran downstairs and got on the phone to Peter Harridance, but got little joy.

'Not a chance of getting anyone out there for the next hour or so, Charlie.'

'Any objection if I go along and have a look?'

'None at all. But Slepton is a small place. Everyone knows everyone else's business, and you stand out. I bet you're well known already as a Leeds copper, and at the sight of you they'll melt away like snow in April.'

Charlie was pretty sure that Nick would be proved right, but the initial signs were encouraging. As he approached the turnoff that the children had taken he heard them giving raucous voice to a variation on their earlier chant.

'Man, man, nowhere man,
Shove a pigstick up his arse,
And chuck him down the pan.'

This was succeeded by cries louder and more disciplined than any he had heard before. He turned up into the estate, but when he made the second turn into Willow Crescent he realised the noise had suddenly ceased, and all he saw were legs and bottoms disappearing around the corner at the far end of the Crescent.

He kept on his way, and stopped outside number thirty-five. Lights were on in the living room and in what was probably the kitchen at the back. No human form was visible. The main door was on the near side of the house, and it seemed to open into an unlit hallway. Charlie rang on the doorbell, then waited in utter silence. He bent down and opened the letter-box.

'Mr Norton! Mrs Norton! I'm a policeman. Inspector Peace. I'd like to talk to you about the children please.'

The silence remained unbroken. He could imagine them cowering in the dark little hall. He tried a second time, with no better result. Then he turned and left the estate where everything was 'new and worked'. Except the human relations, perhaps.

Once home he phoned Directory Enquiries and got the Nortons' number. When he rang it, he was answered cautiously.

'Er ... yes?'

'Mr Norton, my name is Peace. Inspector Peace. I was just round at your house–'

'Oh yes, Mr Peace. Er, Inspector Peace. We didn't want to open the door, in case there were still any children around, and they saw. Telephone is much better.'

'Just as you like, Mr Norton. I'm not a Halifax policeman, by the way. I'm a Leeds one, but I've come to live fairly close to you, in Walsh Street. I'm interested in these children, and wonder why they've fixed on you and your wife for this ... persecution, shall we call it?'

50

'It's that all right! If only we knew why, Inspector, we might be able to make some sense of it. But we don't know, just can't fathom it. You can imagine how upset my wife is. We'd thought of this little place as ideal for our retirement. Now it's like taking up residence in prison, I tell you.'

'You've had no contact with these particular children before?'

'None. We don't recognise any of them.'

'There's nothing in your past that they could take exception to? Anything you've said that's been reported?'

'Good Lord, no. We're not public figures, Inspector. There's no reason why any reporter should get on to anything I've ever said. Anyway, what could it be about? And where could they have seen it, because we're not from round here? I'm not even the sort of person who sounds off about the younger generation. There's good and bad in every generation, that's what I say.'

'You've no criminal record?'

'No, I haven't. You're thinking of paedophiles, aren't you, and the one that was hounded to death in the north-east? No, there's nothing like that, Inspector. It's just ... unbelievable. I tell you, we can't stand much more of it. We've put the house on the market – tactfully, like: no boards up or anything. But if someone came to view, how could we *not* tell them about what's happened and why we're leaving? They'd have a real grievance if they moved here and the same thing happened. I tell you, we're at our wits' ends!'

And Charlie felt the same way, as far as offering any advice or comfort was concerned. He gave them his home phone number, said he'd keep as much of an eye as was possible on how things were going, but in his mind there hung over the whole matter an air of the bizarre, of something totally irrational. Or was he just failing to get into the minds of the children?

He was just slipping into his car next morning when he saw Chris Carlson's car approaching from his home two streets away. The back seat was loaded with an easel and the equipment for a day's painting.

'I don't want to keep you from your art–' began Charlie.

'Sarky bugger.'

'Not at all. It's my kind of art. I just wondered what you know about these children who've been terrorising an elderly couple on the Hatton Estate.'

Chris Carlson frowned. Charlie had the impression he felt he was expected to know pretty well everything that happened in Slepton.

'Nothing at all. I've not even heard about it.'

'That's unusual for you.'

'Maybe it's because it's the estate. The

people there tend to keep themselves to themselves. The younger ones go off to pubs and clubs on the local circuit, and the older ones don't seem to feel the need to go to the pubs here. So what's been going on?'

Charlie told him, and Chris Carlson's expression told of a mixture of interest and bewilderment.

'Three points that interest me,' Charlie ended up, 'are these. First, the Nortons don't recognise the children. That may be because the Nortons are new here, but it seems odd. Then, the children are very well organised by the elder ones. What I heard last night was disciplined chanting and disciplined shouting of abuse. And the third thing is just an oddity: the basis of the chanting seems to be some lines from *The Tempest*, according to Felicity.'

'Ah!' Light seemed to flood into Chris's eyes.

''Ban, 'Ban, Ca-Caliban...'

'Has a new master – Get a new man.'

'That's it. Where would they have come across that in today's schools?'

'Try talking to Harvey Buckworth. He's a teacher. Came up to me with rather an interesting story the other night.'

'The night we were in the pub?'

'I think it may have been.'

'I picked out one of your "patients" as a schoolmaster right away.'

53

'Smartarse.'

'Not at all. Usually when I do that the "schoolmaster" turns out to be an SAS man in mufti. Where does this man teach?'

'That's the interesting thing. He's at Westowram High, a couple of miles down the road. It's where the kids from here go, and it has a very strong drama and stage tradition. Several kids from there have got parts on television – bit parts in police dramas, or long-term child parts in soaps. Harvey is part of the drama set-up, part of its great success. But he's worried.'

'What about?'

'I'd better let him tell you that, hadn't I? And perhaps get you a look at the class that's doing *The Tempest*. I'll arrange it. Harvey will be keen to talk to you. I'll phone you tonight.'

And raising his hand he went off to capture on canvas Bolton Abbey or Haworth moors or the main street of Heptonstall, happy as a sandboy with his life of fulfilment and liberation.

4

Children

Charlie's next few days were taken up with work – work that seemed non-stop and utterly exhausting – after a uniformed sergeant was severely injured in a shooting incident in the centre of Leeds. Charlie's involvement with affairs at Slepton Edge was restricted to talking about them with Felicity over a nightcap, or in bed. The talking was a relief and a change, but it did not notably advance them in the ticklish matter of Rupert Coggenhoe and his curiously abrupt departure from his former home. He remained in their lives an unknown quantity and an unlovely figure, now more than ever surrounded by question marks and even by downright mystery.

'I still can't face the prospect of ringing round and trying to find out what went on down in Coombe Barton,' Felicity said to a near-totally exhausted Charlie. 'In the papers you read nothing these days but lectures about ageism and the old needing their independence and their dignity.'

'Your father has always had a surplus of

dignity,' said Charlie.

'It's not dignity, it's prickliness. But all this newspaper talk about dignity just paralyses me. A niggling little voice tells me I ought to be challenging him, getting him to explain himself, tell us what went on. But I can't.'

'Quite apart from the fact that you wouldn't be told the truth,' Charlie pointed out. This undoubted fact stymied Felicity, who had been about to suggest that since he spent much of his professional life ferreting around in other people's private affairs, he would be the best one to challenge her father. Charlie rubbed in his advantage. 'So don't suggest that I take him on, because he'd be just as likely to lie to me as he would to you. More. Because I know him less well and he'd be more likely to think he could put one over on me. Your father is a god-awful human being, but he's not stupid.'

Felicity never gave up easily.

'That is true. But it doesn't apply to Madge Easton. You would be much better at working the truth out of her.'

'Why? I'm used to getting the truth out of suspects and others who are involved on the margins of criminal cases. Madge Easton is a quite different kettle of fish, and most probably a model citizen. She'd be much more likely to talk openly to you.'

'Why?'

'Because you're white, because you're his

daughter, and the one left who is closest to him. You have a claim to know, and I only have any claim at all through being married to you.'

That was so obviously true that it silenced Felicity for a while. When she took the matter up again, she was on quite a different tack.

'I really can't believe it's anything to do with children.'

'Why on earth should it be?' Charlie demanded sleepily.

'He's never shown the slightest interest in under-age girls, not interest of a sexual sort.'

Charlie took some time to digest this.

'Your thought processes are giving me difficulty. Are you thinking of children because of the gang that's persecuting the Nortons? It must be the two things getting jumbled together in your mind if so, because there's no known connection. Or when you said "not of a sexual sort", was it because there *was* some other sort, something less criminal, but a bit unsavoury?'

'Neither criminal nor unsavoury really,' Felicity said. It was a while before she went on. 'He's always loved being the centre of attention as you know. Particularly from women. Attention, shading off into devotion, shading off into discipleship. He got that, discipleship, from mother. It made it very difficult for me to get close to her. I always

57

felt he hoped – expected, even – to get the same from me: the daughter who kept his flame alive and worshipped his memory. But I grew up with him, and by the time I reached puberty I'd seen through him. Good and proper, as you know. It could be that he's looking round for a replacement for the daughter who never came up to scratch.'

Charlie grunted, to show that he'd registered and understood. Some minutes later Felicity said:

'I wonder if this is something we could talk to Chris about.'

But from the other side of the bed there came only the sound of deep breathing. Felicity knew when Charlie was fast asleep.

But perhaps the idea had got through subliminally, or perhaps he had got the idea independently (talking to Chris, after all, was practically an automatic reaction in Slepton Edge when situations of crisis or even mere difficulty cropped up). Because three days later, when miraculously Charlie had got home before six, Chris and Alison dropped in for coffee later in the evening, and as they settled down Charlie, on an impulse, said to Chris:

'Do older men ever suddenly get the need to have children – have them sexually, I mean – when there's never been any suspicion of paedophilia before?'

Chris raised his eyebrows and thought.

'You'd probably know more about that than I would. I never came across a case in my period as a GP. But who knows what's going on in people's thoughts? I just couldn't say.'

'I don't think it's sexual,' said Felicity. 'If that is the problem the reason is his need for admiration, cosseting, unconditional love.'

'I take it that it's your father we're talking about,' said Chris.

'Yes,' said Charlie, stirring his coffee meditatively. 'We've had an indication that he hasn't been entirely honest with us – that he had to leave his cottage in the West Country after some kind of trouble.' He gave Chris a summary of Mrs Easton's letter. 'Felicity has got the idea that the trouble involves young girls, though that's certainly not stated, and to my mind anything else is equally possible: he could have pressured one of the older women, who obviously were doing everything for him in the domestic line, for sex.'

'Does it have to be sexual?' Alison asked. 'Couldn't he have swindled one of the women out of her comfortable nest-egg?'

'He helped us – considerably – to buy this house,' said Felicity, 'on top of buying his own. He's *very* comfortably off – from writing, but mainly a large legacy.'

'When did being comfortably off stop people from wanting more?' asked Alison.

'You've got to face it, Felicity,' said Chris.

'The problems back in wherever-it-is–'

'Coombe Barton.'

'Pure Agatha-Christie land. The problems could be anything: exposing himself in a public place, not paying his tradesmen's bills, spreading malicious gossip, even putting some of the sterling citizens of the village into one of his books. If you fix on young girls, perhaps it's because you're feeling slightly guilty – feeling that you failed him in some way.'

Felicity shook her head at Chris's suggestion.

'I am *not* feeling guilty. If Dad has a need for total admiration, he's the one who should feel guilty. And to a lesser extent my mother, who gave it to him all their married life. She was nothing to him but a doormat, and I feel ashamed of her. I'm proud of myself for seeing through him when I was still a child.'

'OK, OK. But you really know the answer to this, don't you? You have to ring this Mrs Easton and ask her straight.'

'It seems such an invasion of his privacy,' said Charlie.

'That's what it is. So if you're not willing to do that, you'll have to live with uncertainty. That's not so very terrible. Most of us do that all the time, often with people we know well.'

'A policeman hates living with uncertainty,' said Charlie.

'But a policeman has to do it, the same as everyone else, and probably more frequently.'

'Hmmm,' said Charlie, considering. 'I suppose that's why we always say we know who did most of the well-known unsolved crimes. We know who did it, but we can't put together a case that would stand up in court. We don't like facing up to the fact that if we can't put together a strong case, we can't really know who did it.'

The next day the Leeds police hunt for the gunman who had shot the policeman involved Charlie again, and for the next four days. It ended with the arrest of the culprit in a bed-and-breakfast dive in Bolton. It was an appropriately dingy and depressing end to a sad case. And after that came the mountain of paperwork and cross-checking. So it was nearly a week after the earlier conversation with Chris before Charlie could ring Harvey Buckworth, the drama teacher at Westowram High. He was interested and cooperative, as well as a little apprehensive, as most people are at unexpected approaches from the police. He was teaching the class that he thought Charlie might be interested in the first period after lunch next day, and he had a free period for a chat immediately afterwards. He suggested he meet Charlie at the school gates about half past one.

Loitering there next day, Charlie hoped no

one was going to take him for a paedophile. Some of the girls – no, some of the *pupils* – in the playground seemed to be dressed and behaving in a way calculated to attract the wrong kind of attention. Charlie was relieved when he saw Harvey Buckworth approaching from the main building. He knew at once it was him, because he recognised him from seeing him in the Black Heifer. Otherwise he would not have thought him an obvious drama teacher: he was short, bespectacled and quite lacking in charisma. His handshake, however, was firm and welcoming, and there was a spark of vitality in his eyes.

'I think the best idea would be for me to put right out of my mind any knowledge of what you told me over the phone,' Buckworth said. 'As you know, it's not clear what, if any, offence was committed, and it's not clear either what motive or aim there is in what these children are doing.'

'That's fine by me,' said Charlie. 'But why am I supposed to be here?'

'I'll just call you an observer,' said Buckworth, as they began towards the main school building. 'You could be a talent scout from *Emmerdale Farm* or *Corrie*. These children are performers, all of them, and they'll be thrilled that you're here.'

Charlie felt distinctly dubious about this, but kept silent. They entered the school's main building and made for a room that was

62

larger than a classroom but not quite a hall. The desks were all towards the back, making a good-sized playing area at the front. There was no teacher's desk facing the class, merely a chair set a little apart from the desks, from which Buckworth could watch the performers and turn easily to address the rest of the class. Harvey Buckworth gestured Charlie to one of the desks in the back row, which Charlie overfilled, and then Harvey talked to the class from his chair.

'We've an observer with us today,' he said, raising his voice over the moderate din and quelling it, 'so I want you to be on your best behaviour. And to give your best performance.'

Charlie was conscious of faces turned slightly, eyes alert, note being taken of him. He thought that most of them had heard of a black policeman coming to live in the area.

'We'll go back a little,' announced Buckworth, 'to Act II, scene II, and we'll take it up at Stephano's song – "I shall no more to sea". I'll take the first cast today, and we'll go straight through to the end of the scene. Right: Caliban, Trinculo and Stephano.'

Three of the boys went to the acting-space and took up well-rehearsed positions as Stephano began his song about the 'master, the swabber, the boatswain and I'. Caliban, Charlie noticed, was a strong-looking dark-haired white boy of about fifteen. Trinculo and Stephano were smaller and younger, and Trinculo was black. Colour-blind casting. The three boys were surprisingly good at acting drunk – perhaps through watching their parents, perhaps through watching their fellows or themselves. They weaved around the stage waving their bottles with the abandon of a twenty-something on a cheap holiday in Majorca.

'Now get it together,' said Buckworth from the sidelines. 'You've got to get it disciplined before it can be loosened up a bit. Right, from "I'll show thee the best springs: I'll pluck thee berries".'

And the boys shed some of the assumed haziness from drink and came together, naturally enough, in the centre of the stage, as Caliban led them with 'Farewell, master; farewell, farewell' and the three, looking straight into the audience, sang the song Charlie remembered hearing a parody of.

''Ban, 'Ban, Ca-Caliban,
Has a new master – Get a new man.'

'Right, that's fine,' said their teacher. 'But let's start getting it a bit more natural, a bit less disciplined. Don't all look at the same part of the audience. Each of you choose someone to sing the song to, then change to someone else at some point as you go along. Right – from "Farewell, master".'

They began again, this time more of a rabble and less of an army, and as the song progressed some of the audience began to join in – Charlie noticed which ones. By the third repetition the whole class was joining in the song, belting it out with disciplined ferocity. Charlie was impressed by Buckworth's quiet mastery of his talented class. What exactly had worried this teacher so much that he had talked to Chris Carlson about it?

They had gone on to the next scene, Ferdinand carrying logs, observed by Miranda and, from a distance, Prospero. The boy playing Ferdinand did a convincingly sweaty job, but the girl playing Miranda was quite extraordinary. She glowed in her fresh, innocent appreciation of Ferdinand – her voice took to the verse as if it was her playground argot:

'...I would not wish
Any companion in the world but you,
Nor can imagination form a shape,
Besides yourself, to like of.'

Charlie knew her, knew her at once. She was the leader of the little gang who were persecuting the Nortons, one of the older ones. And he knew something else: when she looked into the audience she looked at him, and she knew who he was. It didn't put her off her stride one iota, but she knew he was a policeman, and that he lived in Slepton Edge.

The rehearsal progressed smoothly to its end. The play was clearly half-way ready to be a really notable public production. When Harvey Buckworth called a halt to it there were still five minutes of class time left. He looked interrogatively towards Charlie, who made a swift decision. He had once toyed with the idea of trying to get into drama school. Performing was in his blood, though he knew if he'd taken a role in the rehearsal he had just witnessed he would have acquitted himself embarrassingly beside these talented teenagers. He knew because he had experienced something like envy when he had watched them – young performers, one or two of whom could be poised to start a professional career in the theatre. Still, he had stood up in front of school classes before, and he felt he could even say something to these drama specialists. He got up and went to the front of the class.

'I enjoyed that. And I was impressed by it too,' he said, looking at them. He felt sure he could identify one or two of the younger children he had seen walking past his home. 'I can see how exciting it is, being in a play, and how naturally you all take to it. But there's one thing I don't think some of you have learnt yet.' And he let his eye range around the group, occasionally resting on faces that he recognised. 'Acting is one thing, real life is another. Some actors will take hours before a performance to get into a part, so he or she feels they *are* the character in the play. But even he has to draw a line between being on stage and being off it. Because otherwise the wife of the man playing Othello would be in danger of getting strangled in a fit of jealousy. Or the man sleeping in the spare bedroom of the woman playing Lady Macbeth might be in danger of getting a dagger thrust into his heart. Do you understand what I'm saying? Some of you have been carrying over things you've been acting out here into your everyday lives. And if you were to take it much further than you already have, you might find yourselves in real trouble.

'Thank you for letting me watch you today.'

And joining up with Harvey Buckworth he went down the aisle between the desks and out of the door. But before the door shut he heard a girl's voice say:

'What does he know? He's just a thick black cop.'

He and Buckworth looked at each other.

'Want a chat?' the teacher asked.

'I think so, yes,' said Charlie. 'There are one or two things I don't know.' As they walked towards an empty classroom he said: 'They were pretty impressive.'

'Thank you. They're hand-picked, of course, from the whole school, so I have would-be Thespians of all ages.'

'The girl was fabulous.'

'She is. There was strong competition for

the part, because Shakespeare never has enough women's parts. Anne Michaels was the best of a very promising bunch.'

'She's one of the little group.'

'I guessed that from looking at you.'

'She's the leader, I think.'

They found a classroom and shut themselves in.

'I'm sad about that,' said Buckworth, sitting at a desk. 'But it's probably just a phase: the usual hormonal problems of teenagers magnified in the case of would-be actors. They crave excitement, recognition, status among their peers – it's perfectly natural.'

'Maybe. Tell that to the Nortons when they've got seven or eight of them shouting and chanting outside their living room.'

'What exactly have they been doing?'

Charlie told him, ending up: 'In other words, borderline stuff as far as the police are concerned, but unpleasant and well-organised.'

'Well, at least your little talk should have stopped *that*,' said Harvey. Something in his tone caught Charlie's attention.

'There's a "but" in your voice.'

'But it won't have done anything to rein in the impulses that led to this particular outbreak of activity. They'll find something else to do – either as individuals or as a group. Let's hope those are things that are less unpleasant, less upsetting to the victims.'

'Do there have to be victims?'

'I think there are likely to be. They start seeing themselves as beings apart as soon as they get the drama bug. Ordinary people seem pathetic, contemptible, and therefore good victims.'

Charlie thought for a moment.

'Not good for a school to have kids with attitudes like that. Tell me about the problem that you took to Chris Carlson.'

'Ah yes.' Buckworth's reluctance was palpable. He shifted in his seat, took a deep breath, then began. 'We don't do just one project in our classes. In fact, most of the rehearsals for *The Tempest* take place outside school hours. In regular classes we do movement, dance, elocution – and of course other plays. One of the things the drama stream has been doing has been a radio play. It's by Giles Cooper, and it's called *Unman, Wittering and Zigo*.'

'Come again?'

'It's the last three names on a class register – odd, rather unnerving names, aren't they? My class lists always end with names like Walker, Wilson and Young. But you can see why I thought it a good piece to do, can't you? It's set in a school, with lots of scenes in a classroom, and it's a radio play, so we could concentrate on voice, enunciation, *using* the voice to create character and atmosphere.'

'So what was the problem?'

'The play is what you might call modern Grand Guignol: very creepy, menacing. The class's new teacher gradually realises that the boys have killed the previous master, and are now thinking of killing him too. Splendid stuff, of course...'

'But?'

'It was so close to their own lives, in setting and activities. It was all much more exciting, of course, but yet easily related to everyday life here in school.'

'So what happened? Did they pick on you?'

'No, too easy. I'd have realised at once where it was coming from. They picked on another teacher, the one who took some of them for English. Still fairly young and nervous. Impressionable.'

'What did they do?'

'Harped on the violent death of a teacher. In essays, stories, on the blackboard when he came into class. Pictures of bodies lying in pools of their own blood, bodies with a dagger protruding from the heart, people backed into a corner surrounded by a gang of schoolchildren with knives in their hands. And so on. Not subtle at all, but who wants children to be subtle? He's a young man, married with a young daughter. He got the wind up.'

'I'm not surprised. Did he come to you?'

'Not at once. Not for a long time, in fact. He didn't realise where the idea was coming from. But he kept hearing the names chanted: Unman, Wittering and Zigo. Didn't mean anything to him. Eventually it dawned on him that these had to be literary names, not names they had invented. Not the brightest sparkler in the fireworks box, our Mr Warburton. He realised there was someone else doing literary texts, and he came along and talked to me.'

'So what did you advise?'

'That he made a mild joke of it. I'd talked it over with Chris, and that was his advice. Call the children by the names in the play. Even make a joke about their murder plans, so long as he could do it without making a big thing out of it. It seems to have worked. That's what I was talking about in the pub the other night.'

Charlie tried not to look too sceptical. He didn't doubt that Harvey Buckworth was telling the truth, so far as it went. But his worried expression in the Black Heifer suggested he was already concerned that the children would go on to something else. Perhaps he had known already about Anne Michaels's little gang, but had kept quiet about it to Chris and to him. He didn't give the impression of being a man who would risk his beloved drama stream for a mere matter of principle.

'Yes. Except that the children have gone on to something else.'

'Not necessarily the same kids, of course.'

'Maybe not. The same impulses though. You've more or less said the same thing yourself.'

Buckworth shot him a glance, not altogether friendly.

'I'm anxious not to let any impression get around that the specialisation on drama and show business we have in the school releases all sorts of undesirable emotions and impulses better damped down. There are plenty of teachers in the school who would like us to restrict ourselves to the three Rs. In fact, they're jealous of our success – we have put the school on the map.'

'And you want to keep it there?'

'Of course I do. OK, I confess it: every time I see one of our kids on *Emmerdale* or wherever I get a glow of pride, a kick. It makes the whole caboodle worth while.'

He didn't add that teaching drama was a hell of a lot more exciting and fulfilling than teaching spelling and punctuation to 2C. That never got anyone into the papers.

'Then you'd better get busy, hadn't you?' Charlie said, with a touch of brutality in his tone. 'Put a stop to all the extracurricular activities that the drama course has led to. It's up to you now, isn't it?'

Harvey looked at him, apparently bewildered.

'But I don't understand. What can I do?

What they do in their own time isn't something I can control.'

'You seem to have given good advice to Mr Warburton. I should have thought a strong, clear message that these outside off-shoots of their drama classes here are putting the very existence of the course in danger would have some effect. The children obviously love being in the drama stream.'

'Of course they do. It's their favourite period of the day, by miles.'

'Naturally it is. It appeals to the exhibitionist in them. That's why reality TV is so popular: it's any exhibitionist's dream. Well, your problem is, you've got to harness the dramatic urge in the classroom, and stamp it out when the school day finishes. I'm sure your courses have been wonderfully successful. But the danger is that they've been *too* successful, and have taken over their lives. That's the problem you've got to deal with, Mr Buckworth.'

And Charlie turned on his heels and left him. Uneasily, but he didn't see what else he could do. Buckworth was the only person who had regular contact with the children. He had the ultimate carrot to dangle in front of them – the continuance of the course they loved, and the dream of parts on stage or in TV productions in the future. Charlie did not see that he could do anything, officially or unofficially, beyond what he had already done.

The next day, arriving home dead on his feet after a twelve-hour shift, he heard from a distance the sound of the Caliban song. He got the idea that it came from a new direction, not from the Hatton Homes Estate, as before, but roughly from the direction of Forsythia Avenue where Rupert Coggenhoe lived. But he was fit for nothing, he forgot the impression, and he shut himself into his home with Felicity and Carola, otherwise dead to the world.

5

Dad

Charlie's work on the case of the wounded Leeds policeman kept him busy throughout the next weekend, but then began to tail off. Someone was in custody – the right man, Charlie was convinced – and the putting together of a case was something of a nine-to-five job. After the days of stacked-up overtime, he had the weekend entirely free, and he and Felicity planned to do something with Carola, perhaps go to one of the pre-Christmas events in the Piece Hall, that glorious survival from Halifax's days at the centre of the wool trade. But before that, something had to be done, Felicity had decided: he found when he got home on Friday afternoon that she had steeled herself to do what she had always known she was going to have to do.

'I'm going to ring Mrs Easton tonight,' she announced over coffee. 'I'm ready at last.'

'Good. About time,' said Charlie.

'Will you take Carola out somewhere, so I can have the house to myself?'

Charlie raised his eyebrows, mystified.

'Why? What's the point? She's usually pretty good if we're on the phone.'

'I want both of you out. Particularly you. I don't want to be self-conscious. I don't want you listening in and saying I handled it badly.'

'Would I?'

'You might be thinking it. And I'd probably think you were thinking it.'

'Hmmm,' said Charlie, draining his cup. 'The return of your father into our lives is not working out well. Soon you'll be back to the poor little girl without confidence you were when we met in Micklewike.'

'Oh *don't*,' said Felicity, her tone heartfelt.

It was easy, in the early evening, to persuade Carola to come for a walk up to Chris and Alison's. She liked the couple, she liked the apparatus of painting, she liked giving her opinion about the results, she liked

Chris's computer, Internet and websites. Above all she liked the fact that Alison was pregnant like her mother, and the pair of babies that would result could be the subjects of infinite speculation.

'Will the babies be twins?' she asked. It was obviously a question she had been preparing on the way there, and it was accompanied by a gentle poke at Alison's belly.

'No, they won't, Carola,' said Alison, though she had a suspicion that Carola knew the answer to her question perfectly well. 'Twins always have the same mummy. Our baby will probably look a bit like me or Chris, or perhaps some of its grandparents, and your mummy's baby will look either like her or your daddy, or perhaps a grandparent.'

This was a new idea to Carola, who pondered.

'Well, if he looks like Grandad I'm not having anything to do with him,' she declared. Charlie's parentage was undetermined on the male side, so there was no doubt who she was talking about. Rupert Coggenhoe was not a hit with his only grandchild. She didn't take kindly to being ignored.

Charlie was in conversation with Chris over by the computer. One of Chris's time-killing amusements was to send idiotic questions to *The Times*'s Questions Answered columns, then wait for idiotic or ignorant replies. That day he was delighted because one of his questions had got into the morning's papers.

'It's the *only* way I waste time on the Internet, and it serves as a reminder how easy it is to waste hour after hour on it.'

'You're being unusually defensive,' said Charlie. 'So what was the question today, then?'

'Who was Tom the piper's son, and why did he run away with a pig?'

Charlie considered.

'Do you know, that's something I've never felt the need to give a lot of thought to.'

'All the better. We'll get a lot of answers from people who never have either, but who think up stupid answers on the spur of the moment.'

'Couldn't you go to a book about nursery rhymes?'

'If you really wanted an answer you could. If there was an answer at all.'

'I don't see why you want to associate yourself with those idiots who spend hour upon hour on this sort of nonsense.'

'It reminds me that at some stage I'm going to want to do a really useful job again. And that I should soon start to think about what it is likely to be.'

Charlie nodded.

'They say doctors do pretty useful work,' he said.

'Mrs Easton?'

'Ye-e-es.'

'This is Felicity Peace.' Puzzled silence at the other end. 'Rupert Coggenhoe's daughter.'

There was an audible intake of breath.

'Oh yes. I remember now. And your husband is Charlie, isn't he? I couldn't remember when I sent your father's...'

Her voice trailed off. Unable to mention vests and underpants, Felicity wondered? Or a different kind of embarrassment? There was something odd about the response: the words seemed friendly enough, but not the tone. Or was it simply uncertain?

'It was kind of you to send them,' she said. 'But I was a little bit worried about your letter. I didn't want to take it up with you, but in the end I couldn't think of anything else I could do.'

'Oh, it wasn't my intention to worry you.'

'But perhaps it was your intention to warn me?'

There was silence for a moment. Mrs Easton's voice had sounded flustered, and now Felicity's remark seemed to have touched a chord.

'Well, maybe, yes. I don't think people should be haunted for ever and ever for just one mistake – don't think that. But if it can happen down here, it can happen up there too, because your father's the same man... I didn't want to go into details.'

'No, I could see that from the letter. But perhaps your not wanting to go into details has meant that I've been more anxious than I've needed to be. For example, I don't know what to look out for, so I look out for every little thing. Of course I know my father very well in many ways, but I did get away – I mean *move* away from home – quite a long time ago now. People change, situations change. That's why I feel I need to know precisely what it was that happened down there, what the trouble was, and why he moved away so quickly, pretending he had made a quick sale of his cottage.'

Mrs Easton once again seemed to think over her response. She had probably half expected a phone call immediately after sending the letter, but the expectations had faded.

'Yes, I can see that you need to know. And after all the talk is all over Coombe Barton.'

'I thought it probably was. Please don't worry about upsetting me. My father and I have never been very close. You may have guessed that, as we never visited. I never cared about him because he never cared about me. It's just a question of *knowing*, of having some idea what I should be trying to nip in the bud. That is, if there is the slightest possibility of that, with my dad.'

'Yes, I can see he won't be easy to persuade... Well, it all started with the death of your mother.'

'I had a pretty good idea that would be when it started.'

'We all liked your mother. She was very supportive of your father, and so she should have been. She could smooth down any rough edges – because you know he has a high opinion of himself, and what is due to him.'

'I know it.'

'So when she died we all rallied round, one helping with this, another with that – shopping, cleaning, cooking, even gardening, just until he found his feet, you know.'

'I know. Only he never found them.'

'Well, that's right... One or two of us had to say eventually: "It's time you learnt to do this for yourself."'

'Did it work?'

Mrs Easton gave a little nervous laugh.

'Well, it had to, if we weren't willing to go on being his sl– servants. But there were some who weren't strong-minded enough to simply stop helping. And they tended to get – put upon still more. I'm being brutally frank.'

'Understating things, I'd be willing to bet.'

'Yes, well... There was – is – one lady, Dora Catchpole, who'd done most of his cleaning for him since your mother's death.'

'Unpaid?'

'Oh yes, of course! None of us would have thought of accepting payment.' There was shock in the voice. It was obviously a very important class matter for Mrs Easton. Only the lack of payment made it more difficult to hand in your notice. 'Anyway, Dora took on not just the scrubbing and vacuuming – he likes things just so, doesn't he, your dad? – but bits of shopping and laundry. Those two items I sent' (even now she couldn't bring herself to specify their nature) 'came from her. And it was a lot for her to do, being a widow with a part-time job, and so sometimes she took along her granddaughter, just to give a hand like, at the start.'

Eventually Felicity had to say the word 'And', just to break the silence.

'Well, Kylie's a nice girl, nearly fifteen, always got her nose in a book, no close friends, rather plain – lovely eyes, but the lads don't bother much with eyes, do they? And she went along to the cottage to do bits and bobs to help her granny, but also because she was over the moon at getting to know a real writer. She read everything in the library by him, looked up to him, all breathless. Embarrassing to think of, isn't it, the sort of things we did at that age? I had a thing about clergymen. But of course your father should have tried to cool things down. Everyone thought that.'

'But instead he accepted all the adoration?'

'Yes. Called her "My little Princess" and "My Muse", read her what he was writing at the moment, used her name in the book for a fascinating young woman character. There's not many girls of that age wouldn't let that sort of thing go to their heads.'

'No, I can see that. It should never have been offered to her in the first place.'

'It shouldn't. That's what Dora Catchpole thought, though she kept it to herself at first. She went on with the work, but she got very unhappy about Kylie's emotional state, and she had a few words with her daughter and son-in-law, playing it down a little. But the question kept nagging her: what was it going to lead to? Any mother or relative would have been uneasy.'

'I can see that.'

'So of course she stopped bringing the girl, and he'd ask "Where's Kylie?" and she'd say she had a lot of homework, or a school project, or was taking swimming lessons. Eventually she realised she would have to tell him the truth. It was a day when she'd spent several hours giving the house a good going over, to salve her conscience I expect. She was just off home, and in the hallway he stopped her and said: "Be sure to bring Kylie next time." She expected it, because he was saying it all the time. She took a deep breath and said the parents weren't happy about the situation – which they weren't, but it was really herself she was talking about. She said with children that age relationships could get a bit more serious than was intended. It was a crucial time, with her exams coming up, and her parents thought it was time for her to stop coming up to the cottage with her granny and knuckle down to real work with her friends (though as I say she hadn't got any what you'd call friends, which was part of the problem).'

'What did he say?'

'It wasn't what he said, it was what he did.'

Felicity's heart missed a beat.

'Tell me.'

'He hit her... What you might call a cuff. A heavy cuff across the head. Then he swore at her. Poor Dora ran for her life.'

'So you've decided you want to enter the real work-force again,' said Charlie to Chris.

'Decided? No, we haven't decided, have we, darling?'

He pushed the computer screen away from him and turned to his wife.

'Not *decided*,' said Alison. 'Life is too pleasant as it is.'

'It's useful too, in its way, isn't it?' asked Charlie.

'Maybe, in its little way,' said Chris. 'Listening to tales of illness, mostly imaginary, trying to sift through and find the real ones that could need treatment. Persuading Desmond Pinkhurst that his whole life as an actor has been a preparation for taking the part of Old Ekdal in *The Wild Duck*.'

'I was told he went off to Sheffield for the rehearsals as happy as a sandboy.'

Chris shrugged.

'But I'm a doctor. I could sense the pit of fear in his stomach. I've had a postcard saying he's enjoying rehearsals immensely. But I can't judge postcards, only people.'

'The point is,' said Alison, 'that we're waiting for the birth of the son and heir, and when that's past us and we've breathed a sigh of relief, then we'll start thinking.'

Charlie put on his experienced-family-man look.

'The birth of a first child is *just* the time when a demanding job seems least inviting. I used to begrudge the time spent on the most exciting and interesting cases.'

'Then we'll put off the decision for a year or two. There's always a demand for doctors,' said Chris confidently, 'and we could go to Haiti or Mozambique or wherever – *really* poor places – if we wanted to do a useful job.'

'Meanwhile you're the eyes and ears of Slepton Edge,' said Charlie, 'and its conscience as well. Have you learnt anything more about that gang of children who've been terrorising the retired couple in Willow Crescent?'

'No, not really,' said Chris, rubbing his chin. 'I wouldn't have thought they were active any longer. Haven't heard that rather aggressive song they sing. But then, we're a fair way away from Willow Crescent.'

'What about Forsythia Avenue?'

'Fors–? Oh – where Felicity's dad lives. Why?'

'Just an idea,' said Charlie hurriedly. 'I came home tired, only wanting to sleep. I heard the song, or imagined I did, but definitely not from the Hatton Homes Estate, where Willow Crescent is. I had the idea at the time that it was roughly from the Forsythia Avenue area.'

'That's only two or three streets away from here. We could have been out, or in with the television or radio on. We wouldn't necessarily have heard it... Alison, doesn't that cop who takes the self-defence classes you go to live in Forsythia Avenue? Ben Costello?'

'I can't remember. Or Luddenden Avenue possibly. Up there somewhere.'

'I wouldn't have thought the kids would start in on anyone if they knew there was a policeman living nearby.'

Charlie laughed out loud.

'You want to bet? You must be still living in the Thirties. When I went to talk to Harvey Buckworth's drama class, one of the girls referred to me as a "thick black cop" in my hearing. And she intended me to hear, I could tell that.'

'That's a bit different. Often the school environment makes them feel safer, whereas gang behaviour on the streets takes a lot more chutzpah. And Ben Costello is a tough-style cop.'

'Well, I'll take your word for it. I didn't want to think that the gang had turned its attention on Rupert, to add to all his and our problems. But he is an incomer, from the bottom end of the country like the Nortons, he's made himself conspicuous, and he's quite incapable of making himself liked.'

'So your visit to the drama class didn't go too well, then?' asked Chris.

'Oh, I think I got the message across. And one thing Buckworth and the kids care about is if the drama stream is threatened. All those child-star jobs on stage and TV gone for a burton. He cares, they care. I think they'll all be a bit more careful from now on.'

'So what happened next?' Felicity asked Mrs Easton, after a pause to let the sinking feeling in her stomach disappear.

'What you'd expect in a little place like this. Dora Catchpole was very upset: she'd been screwing herself up to say what she did say, but the last thing she thought could happen was violence. She'd thought there might be a fit of self-righteousness, or a huff, something like that. When she ran from the house she was crying, and very embarrassed, so on the way home – more as a sort of refuge, a way of hiding herself for a bit so she could pull herself together – she dropped in on one of her friends, whose house happened to be on her way home.'

'And she happened to be the biggest gossip in Coombe Barton,' hazarded Felicity.

'Well, something like that. There's competition for the title. But Dora poured out her heart, felt much better for it, vowed she'd never go back to the cottage–'

'I should have thought that went without saying.'

'Yes, it should. But some people are very silly about things like that, and everyone was very pleased she wasn't being. Anyway, the upshot was she went home feeling much better, and within the hour the story started to spread through the village.'

'I can imagine. How did Dad react?'

Mrs Easton gave a bitter little laugh.

'How could he? He had to start doing his own shopping, and all he got was the cold shoulder. Even shopkeepers were pretty tight-lipped. In the pub no one would talk to him – to tell you the truth that was no great hardship, because most people thought he was a tremendous bore. So he had to face the fact that his cleaning, cooking, gardening and the rest were only going to get done if he did them himself.'

'So they all took Mrs Catchpole's side?'

'What other side was there to take?'

'Of course – I wasn't meaning to imply sympathy for my dad. I don't think I've ever had that in my life. All I was thinking of was that when he decided to move up north, in with or close to us, he was running away from being the Coombe Barton pariah. And he told us he'd made a quick sale and had to get out of the cottage at once.'

'That wasn't true. Oh, you had a lucky escape he didn't decide to move in with you.'

'He didn't decide that. We did. Charlie and I knew that would be the ultimate disaster. Even as it is Charlie was just saying I'm reverting to the pathetic and mixed-up kid I was when he and I first met. Not in those words, but that's what he meant.'

'Oh dear. I hope his moving there hasn't caused trouble in your marriage.'

'Not yet it hasn't, but who knows what may happen later? I was quite pleased when he started getting a little circle of ladies around him, but now the thought terrifies me.'

'Not the same thing over again? Doing everything for him?'

'Not quite the same. There wasn't the same spur to look after him of having known Mum, and realising how hopeless he would be without her. And Yorkshire women are very independent. But if they have a spare hour or two they sometimes go up and see if he's got anything that needs doing. And they give him their company, go to the tea-rooms or the pub with him, hear him pretend to be the world's greatest writer, the world's greatest grandfather, the world's greatest expert on the nature and needs of women.'

'You don't like him much, do you, Felicity?'

'I don't like him at all. Why didn't we say when he first wrote that we wanted nothing to do with him, and certainly didn't want him living near us? I suppose because we welcomed the financial help to buy this house... And also because, well, you *don't* simply repudiate a parent unless you have a whopping good reason for doing it. Usually something in the past. If I ever thought he'd done to my mother what he did to Mrs Catchpole—'

'I never heard anything to suggest that,' said Mrs Easton.

'No. But you wouldn't have. She'd never have told anyone. And from one point of view that's the saddest thing of all. She was just the old-fashioned, complete skivvy and slave, unquestioning, admiring, a real "Yes-sir-no-sir" wife.'

'He won't find another of those very easily.'

'I hope *not!*' said Felicity.

'I'm afraid telling you what happened here will have upset you. And it won't have solved your problem.'

'How could it? But it's told me what my problem is.'

In the half hour before Charlie and Carola came back from the Carlsons' Felicity pottered around the house doing everything and nothing and pondering the new situation which her conversation with Mrs Easton had brought about. Part of her regretted her closing remark. She now knew what *the* problem was, but why had she said that it was *her* problem? It was her father's problem and no one else's.

Because who could do anything about it other than him? There was never any question of his being influenced by her. If she showed him that she knew what had happened in Coombe Barton he would be incandescent with rage, but it would have no effect: in his mind he had no doubt rearranged the incident so that blame was put on the shoulders of all the ladies in the village, ganging up against him.

She could of course warn the ladies of Slepton Edge. If he found out, that would have a similar result – a paddy, with fire-works. But did they need warning? She had a feeling they didn't. All the ladies who offered the occasional meed of help to her father struck her as knowing what they were doing, and as basically canny types who had him summed up. Or was this a hope rather than an assessment?

When Charlie and Carola got home there was bedtime for Carola, a story for her, and then, eventually, blessedly, a late-night drink with Charlie and the chance to tell him everything Mrs Easton had revealed about why her father had fled to Yorkshire.

'Dark Deeds at Coombe Barton,' said Charlie when she had finished. 'A good title for Rupert when he is in Gothic mood.'

'You're not taking it seriously,' Felicity protested.

'Oh, I am, but I'm not taking it *too* seriously. Hitting a woman is bad, but he'd be let off with a caution if she had reported him. Attaching an impressionable teenager to him is a bit off, *potentially* serious. But there's no evidence that anything was done, or even on the cards. As you say, all his women here seem pretty sensible. I bet most of them have got his measure and have talked it through among themselves. And as a consequence they'll be too worldly-wise about dangers to take children or grand-children with them when they go up to Rupert's. Let's face it: Dora Catchpole was a fool to do it. We've heard nothing like that up here to date, and no hint that in general he's attached to little girlies. Let's stop making a mountain about what is basically a molehill.'

As a consequence Felicity let him lead her on to talking about where in Halifax they'd take Carola over the weekend, and she went to bed much happier. In a fool's paradise, but happier.

6

Adeste Fidelis

The carol service at St Wilfrid's, Slepton's parish church, took place on the first Saturday in December. It was the first in a series of Christmas events, and by far the most popular. The church was just off the village square, and it had late-medieval bits to which had been added some fairly appropriate Victorian bits. Few members of the congregation were entirely sure which bits were which, and nobody really cared: by now all of it was 'old'. By tradition (a strong power in Slepton Edge) the first half of the carol service was held outside, and if the weather was anything like appropriate there was mulled wine and non-alcoholic hot drinks served in the winter cold, before everyone went into the church for the second part. 'What you spend on the mulled wine you save on heating,' said the vicar cheerfully, his annual joke, expected and responded to as an old friend.

Felicity and Charlie were intending to go if possible: they tried to be at every village 'thing', as part of the integration process, one that they liked and that everyone else joined in with spirit. In any case, they had no choice because Carola insisted on going: two little girls from her nursery school were going to be Christmas tree fairies, and Carola was determined to cast a critical eye on their dresses, wands and general demeanour.

'Going to nursery school has transformed Carola's life,' said Felicity to Nancy Stoppard, her father's widow-friend. 'She now has a circle of her own.'

'To dominate,' added Charlie. 'She already has them lining up when she arrives, saluting her and shouting "Hail Carola!"'

'They don't say "Hi Carola",' said their daughter scornfully. 'We all say "hello" to each other, and "goodbye" when school is over. Oh look, there's Victoria and Wendy.'

That kept her quiet for the next ten minutes. The two little girls were stationed on either side of the brilliantly-lit Christmas tree, waving their wands with decreasing enthusiasm.

Elsewhere the lights around the church and in the road beyond were more dispersed, in some places bright, in others romantically dim, casting a glow of glamour or mystery over the familiar faces of the village. Little knots of people were on the pavement beyond the church gate under the one street light. Others gathered around the graves or by the main door, waiting for the music to begin, greeting the vicar, and quietening impatient offspring.

'This will be your first carol service at Slepton, won't it?' said Nancy, who had the air of not being entirely easy with them, while doing her duty by village newcomers. 'I always love it – there's something magical about it.'

'We're all looking forward to it,' said Felicity. 'Especially Carola, of course... Oh look, there's Desmond! That *is* nice.'

Desmond Pinkhurst was standing by a gravestone, his legs somehow intertwined, looking about as relaxed as Bertie Wooster at a World Congress of Aunts. But when he saw he had been noticed he brightened up and ambled over.

'I say, isn't this jolly? I always love it. Brings back my own childhood – I once played Joseph, my very first dramatic role! This sort of thing makes the whole ghastly business of Christmas worthwhile. I wonder if Chris will be here,' he went on, looking around him in the way that he had. 'I'm not even sure if he's a Christian. I wanted to thank him for pushing me into taking the part in *The Wild Duck*... You too, of course,' he added, remembering his manners and turning back to Charlie.

'Oh, I only said what everyone would say: Go for it. I'm sure Chris says these things with much more force and experience behind him.'

'Well, of course in a way he... Anyway, you were both right.'

'Oh, we're really glad,' said Charlie and Felicity together.

Desmond rubbed his hands with glee.

'I'm enjoying myself to bits! We've got four days off now, without rehearsals, to stop us getting stale. I can't imagine getting stale in a play like that, but there you are. Then we've got an intensive week until the first night. I say, isn't it a wonderful idea to put it on for *Christmas?*'

'I don't really know,' said Charlie. 'I've never seen it or read it. Is it Christmassy and jolly?'

'Oh, not at all,' said Desmond. 'That's why it's such a clever idea. It's terribly *meaty*, all sorts of levels or layers or whatever in it, and people need an antidote to all those Aladdins and Peter Pans and non-stop *Railway Children* on television. I tell you, the advance bookings are marvellous. Everyone's flabbergasted. A bit of angst and gloom and being made to *think* seems to be just what people need. And want too!'

'I'm really glad,' said Felicity. 'So the part wasn't beyond you after all?'

Desmond put on a coy face.

'Well–' slyly, '–people say not. In fact, they're being *very* kind. And it's a wonderful cast all round. Not just people who've been on the telly, which is so demeaning if you

95

haven't. And my telly days are so long ago that nobody's seen me. Oh – there's Chris.'

Charlie looked at his departing back.

'I feel I'm in a replay,' he said.

'A what?' asked Nancy.

'A replay. A repeat of what happened when Desmond first got offered the Ibsen. He makes do with us, practises his woes and worries or joys and successes on us, then at the first glimpse of Chris he hares off.'

'Chris usually has that effect on people,' said Nancy. Then after a pause she said: 'I wonder if he's heard.'

But before they could ask what he might or might not have heard, the sound of the first carol floated over from the knot of people around the main door. Accompanied by a pumped-up string quartet of local players the church choir and all the assembled locals launched into 'Away in a Manger', and on cue a spotlight illuminated a part of the graveyard with waiting space where a makeshift manger had been set up with children miming the Holy Family (with a doll as the baby, the vicar having vetoed the real thing).

'Very nice,' said Charlie, as the last verse faded.

'It *is* nice,' said Nancy, pleased at his pleasure, and opening up. 'It's pretty much the same every year, but that's because it's lovely, and we want to see it again.'

'What were you wondering whether Chris

had heard or not?' asked Charlie, always the dog gnawing at a bone.

'Oh – about Archie Skelton.'

'Skelton. Isn't he the mayor?'

'That's right. He's had another heart attack.'

'Serious?'

'Very. Couldn't be more.'

Charlie put on a concerned expression and nodded.

The choir and musicians began 'While Shepherds Watched' and the audience's eyes went back to the pretty manger as shepherds came from the side entrance to the church, scantily clad in shifts and carrying crooks in their hands. They paid their respects to the Saviour rather briskly, and then legged it back to the comparative warmth of the church, probably on orders from their parents.

'If I still had a kid to perform in this I'd insist he was a Wise Man,' said Nancy. 'At least you get robes, and you can put a hot water bottle in your casket.'

'They don't look anything like the shepherds on our Christmas card,' said Carola disparagingly. Their first Christmas card had arrived, from a retired bobby Yuletiding it in Spain, and it had become the pattern for Carola's view of the Christmas story.

'Have you heard?' came Chris Carlson's voice suddenly in Charlie's ear.

'What about? Archie Skelton?'

'No, *not* Archie Skelton. About Desmond. He's happy as a sandboy. He's apparently having a whale of a time at rehearsals, and everyone agrees he's doing a fine job.'

'Yes, so he told us.'

Down in the little square of empty lawn 'We Three Kings' signalled the slow arrival into the nativity story of three very dignified small boys, robed and crowned and no doubt warmer than the shepherds as Nancy had said, carrying their caskets very close to their tummies. When their acts of homage were finished, as the carol about them ended too, a further piece of mime showed the Holy Family being warned of King Herod's primitive idea of family planning. There being no carol about the Massacre of the Innocents they all launched into 'O Come, All Ye Faithful' and the little family set off through the gravestones to disappear out of the lighted area. It was interval time, and there was a scramble towards the tables set out beside the front door of the church, with mulled wine, Christmas cake and homemade biscuits.

'Wait a bit,' said Chris, putting out his hand to prevent them starting with the rush. 'The scrum eases quite soon, and there will still be plenty of time to gulp and guzzle before the second half.'

'Is your father here?' Nancy asked Felicity.

She looked vaguely around.

'I've no idea. He's terribly independent these days, thanks to you and to his other new friends here. You may have noticed that he's not awfully into children, whatever he may say, so I didn't ask him to come with us in case he preferred to come with some of you, or stay away altogether.'

'I'll look for him and see that he's all right,' said Nancy, scurrying away into the thirsty mob.

'Implied criticism,' said Felicity.

'Don't you believe it,' said Chris. 'Nancy has scaled down her time commitment to your father herself. But on occasions like this she likes to be of use, and that way she shares in the credit for the success of the evening... There you are: she's found him already. She's joined the throng of fans.'

They watched Rupert Coggenhoe. He was towards the back of the queue, surrounded by a posse of middle-aged or older women, the little group now being joined by Nancy. Slowly, the women chatting happily, Rupert looking benign but out of things, they moved down towards the mulled wine.

'They're losing interest,' said Felicity. 'Scaling down their time commitment as you call it. You can tell from the body language. They're not looking at Dad adoringly as they used to.'

'That's perfectly normal and understandable,' said Chris. 'A newcomer arrives in a village, and for a time he's the centre of everyone's attention, and then they find out that he's really not all that interesting.'

'Don't let my father hear you say that,' said Felicity. 'He'd be livid.'

'Actually,' said Charlie, who had been observing the whole group and taking in the interaction, 'if you look at him closely his eyes are going everywhere now. *He's* not all that interested in *them* if they're not interested in him.'

All their eyes went towards Rupert Coggenhoe. As the queue advanced on the steaming vessel the great author's eyes were indeed, though cautiously, going everywhere. From some signs of irritation among the group of women it was clear his attention was far from any of them, and from anything they said to him.

'He's looking for someone,' said Charlie, unafraid to state the obvious. At that moment Coggenhoe's peripatetic gaze began to steer in their direction, and they hastily looked away.

Felicity swung round to look at Charlie.

'I don't want to see,' she said. 'I don't want to know who it is. I wish we'd never gone along with his plans to move near us. It was just a typical scheme of his to bribe us with his help with the mortgage so that he'd secure a prop for his declining years.'

'Say slave,' said Charlie. 'That's what he wants and that's what he won't get. And don't pretend to be so surprised. We talked over the probability of this as soon as we got the offer, and we said then there were going to be strict limits to our involvement with him.'

'You're both very hard,' said Chris. 'After all, he may not have all that long to go–'

'Oh, don't give me that,' snarled Felicity. 'Have you seen him having trouble walking, have you noticed his mind wandering, have you smelt any signs of incontinence?'

'Well, no, but–'

'He'll live to be a hundred,' said Charlie gloomily. He turned to Chris. 'And talking about not having long to go, you were right about Archie Skelton.'

'I was.'

'I didn't notice you squeezing the tear-ducts for sympathy when you first mentioned to us that Archie was a candidate for a heart attack.'

'I wasn't close to Archie, and nor were you. Like it or not, you are to Rupert.'

'We are *not*,' said Charlie and Felicity together. Chris shrugged.

'Sad.'

'Not sad at all,' said Felicity firmly. 'Perfectly natural. As Swift said, "children aren't obliged to feel gratitude to their parents because when they were being made the parents were thinking of something else entirely".'

'In my mother's case I should think it was whether she had any oven chips in the fridge,' said Charlie. 'She took so little interest in the whole business that she's never been able to remember the name of the man whose efforts made me.'

'Anyway, we have a dead mayor,' said Felicity. 'I suppose what everyone will want to know is whether you're thinking of standing again.'

Chris shrugged – a lack of interest that didn't quite convince.

'I don't know. I've only just heard... I did quite well last time, didn't I? I think the whole idea of an elected mayor is still in the experimental stage, so they could decide to revert to the old way of doing things: nominate an elderly party hack as a reward for always voting at his party's call and never thinking for himself at all. And that probably makes sense: making it elected only brought us the same result – a hack.'

'But it nearly brought us you,' said Felicity.

'I must say you seem to have done quite a lot of thinking in a very short time,' commented Charlie. Chris looked slightly embarrassed.

'Well, to be honest it was something I've been expecting. I more or less told you that when we first met.'

'So you should be able to come to a quick decision.'

'You think so?' Chris scratched his head in comic bewilderment. 'There are so many imponderables. By the time they have made the decision to keep it as an elected post the baby could have arrived, but do babies and campaigning for a job go together? Is this the sort of worthwhile thing that I'm looking for? I'll really have to ponder it a lot, talk it over with Alison... Oh, there she is. Let's all go over and join the queue.'

The queue was down to five or six people. The ones who had been served were clustered in little knots around the main door and out into the graveyard, talking, sipping, laughing.

'Oh look, there's Ben Costello,' said Chris, as they all clutched mugs and biscuits. 'I think you both ought to know him – I'm surprised you don't, Charlie. He's a policeman.'

'My main contact with the station here is a man called Harridance,' said Charlie. He and Felicity let themselves be dragged over to a dark man with slicked-back hair and piercing mauve eyes. There was a lot of gym-muscle about him, and a general air of no-nonsense copper. Alison Carlson raised her hand in greeting to an old friend.

'Ben,' she said, 'this is Charlie Peace – Dexter Peace to his birth certificate – who's come to live in Slepton. And this is his wife

Felicity. Chris over there you know.'

Ben shook hands genially.

'Ah – I'd heard we had refugees from Headingley. Things are getting tough there, aren't they? Every square inch taken over by students. Good to meet you. Coppers either have the instinct to settle down and become part of the community they police, or else the instinct to get away from it so that they're not faced with local villains the whole time. I don't need to ask which category you're in.'

'Definitely. No job ought to be a twenty-four hour one. I've come here to live to see what class of villain you breed, and how it compares with the Leeds variety.'

'I think you'll find they're pretty similar. I'm not local, though. You can probably hear I'm closer to your old haunts than to Yorkshire. I'm Stratford East.'

'And I'm Brixton.'

'And why did you pull up stumps and move north?'

'The instinct you just talked about. Wanting to get away from the people I'd known since birth, from the job, and generally to have a normal off-duty life. And you?'

'Pretty much the same, I suppose.'

'Don't try talking about not wanting a twenty-four hour job if you meet up with a doctor called out in the middle of the night,' said Chris.

'Don't talk crap,' said Ben Costello. 'You all have agency cover these days, and fair enough too.'

'Did you hear about us from my father-in-law?' Charlie asked him.

'Father-in-law? No, I don't think I know him. It was one of our local men, Harridance, that mentioned you. Good man. Safe pair of hands. Oh, here's my wife. Belle, this is Charlie and Felicity, and Alison over there. Chris you know.'

They all smiled at a plump, smiling but forceful-looking woman, exuding confidence, who shook hands with them.

'My father-in-law lives near you both,' said Charlie. 'I thought you might have noticed him as a new arrival – passed him in the street or driven past him.'

'Oh my God,' said Felicity. 'There he is over there.' The words seemed to have been forced out of her – there was a note of drama and foreboding in her voice. All the other eyes in the group followed hers, surprised.

They had shifted position slightly when Belle Costello had joined the group, and they now had a view through the big oaken doors into the body of the church. Rupert Coggenhoe was standing, exuding satisfaction and self-love, talking to a girl in school uniform – which she seemed to transform into an ironic contrast with the body inside it, since her face, her carriage, her gestures seemed to proclaim that she was a stunning beauty about to bloom. It was Anne Michaels, Harvey Buckworth's Miranda, the leader of the little group of childish persecutors.

Felicity moved forward, as if in a dream. Her father was so taken up with his new interest that there was no chance of his noticing her. Soon she was in the church and within hearing distance.

'I must go. My mum and dad are down the front, and they'll wonder where I've gone to.'

'But I'll be seeing you again soon?'

''Course you will. Maybe tomorrow. If not, Monday after school.'

And in a flash she reverted to the school kid and scuttled off down the centre aisle. Felicity stopped in her tracks, bowled over by the sheer banality of the exchange. What had she expected? she asked herself. Breathless vows of eternal love? Had her approach prevented their being put into words? She swallowed hard and put herself where her father could not fail to see her.

'Hello Dad. Are you enjoying the show?'

'Felicity!' He turned, awakening from a dream. 'Very much so. Or as much as a practically tone-deaf person can.'

'Who was the girl? Daughter of one of your harem?'

His nose went into the air in irritation.

'I don't have a harem, as you well know.

No – just a friend. You wouldn't want me to depend entirely on you and Charlie for company, would you? You've made that very clear.'

And he stalked off to the most prominent seat he could find, halfway down the church. Felicity looked back to the little knot of people she had left. Chris was looking at her, sympathetically. Ben Costello and his wife were looking at Rupert Coggenhoe, clambering across people's legs to get to the vacant place.

Charlie's eyes were fixed on Ben Costello, one policeman observing another with the insight of an expert, knowing what was going through his mind. He felt kinship with him, even though he didn't feel he'd ever have him as a friend. They were both new in their jobs, both hungry for further promotion, both outsiders in their patches, both having the same policeman's instincts. Charlie saw Ben registering all the nuances of the encounter he had just witnessed, weighing up alternative hypotheses, cataloguing the nuances in this obviously uneasy father-daughter relationship.

Charlie regretted what had happened in the last minute or two, thinking that Felicity had given away a private matter to an outsider.

Felicity was regretting this herself.

7

Quarry

Felicity and Charlie were able to have some words together on the way home from the carol service. Carola had spotted a nursery schoolmate with her parents just ahead of them, and she decided to string along with them and favour them with her critique of the re-enactments, in particular the Christmas tree fairies, whom she was desperately jealous of. Her parents welcomed the chance to talk alone.

'I know I stuffed it up,' said Felicity despairingly. 'You don't have to tell me.'

'I'm not sure I want to, or that you did,' said Charlie. 'You made Ben Costello suspicious. I could almost see his policeman's nose twitching. But is that necessarily a bad thing? If your father got a hint of police interest in his little flirtation, if that's what it is, it could give him pause for thought.'

'More likely than anything *I* might do or say would do that,' agreed Felicity. 'But, you know, I don't believe there's anything going on. I don't believe he's bedding her, or that he did that with the girl back in Coombe

Barton. I don't believe he even wants to. The danger lies in what other people think is going on.'

Charlie shrugged.

'You know him best. If it's not sex, what is it?'

'Vanity,' said Felicity firmly. 'With him everything comes back to vanity. In the unlikely event of his writing a bestseller, he'd be absolutely unbearable.'

'He's well on the way to being that now,' said Charlie. 'The question is: what do we do?'

They walked on for some time without anything occurring to either of them.

'There's the girl's parents,' said Felicity. Charlie thought about it.

'That would really put the seal on our success as newcomers to the village,' he said at last. 'They no sooner get to know us, start to accept us, than we're warning parents to beware of your father, a man whom we brought with us to Slepton Edge.'

'Not a nice prospect,' agreed Felicity. 'But we can't put our own reputation before what most parents would see as our duty.'

'Except that you don't know there's a sexual danger,' Charlie pointed out.

'No, I don't. And I don't *think* there is. Could I have grown up with a potential paedophile and not have had an inkling? Me? With a novelist's eye already developing? But what a daughter doesn't *think* is happening is not evidence. And there's all sorts of dangers other than sexual ones that parents ought to be warned about.'

'Such as?'

'Making someone of an impressionable age into an acolyte – or is that a boy? Into the keeper of the flame, a besotted fan, a worshipper.'

Charlie raised his eyebrows with a sly grin.

'Somehow I don't recognise anything he could be charged with.'

'Oh, there isn't. Don't be such a typical policeman. There's a whole range of dangerous activities and attitudes that don't come within the criminal code and that parents ought to be warned against.'

'That depends on the parents,' said Charlie thoughtfully. 'Didn't the ones in Devon recognise the dangers and put a stop to their daughter going up to the cottage?'

'Sort of,' said Felicity. 'But I suspect only after a lot of prompting from the grandmother.'

'People always talk about preventative measures,' said Charlie grimly, 'ways of preventing crimes before they happen. I'd just like someone to explain to me what measures there are one can take.'

'Well, stopping their daughter from going to an older man's house seems a reasonable start.'

'I'm beginning to think I would back Anne Michaels against any type of present-day parent I know of,' said Charlie.

The next day was Sunday, and Charlie was in work from early morning. Felicity, though, had an early-morning call from Alison Carlson.

'Are you going to church?' she asked.

'Let me think, wasn't I in church last night?' said Felicity. 'Yes, I was. I wouldn't want to overdo it, Alison. I'm not entirely sure, even, that I'm a Christian.'

'I'm not rounding people up. My aim was entirely social. I thought we might have a talk on the way there or the way back.'

'That would be nice. You can drop in whenever you like.'

'It's just that ... I could see you were upset last night.'

Felicity grimaced.

'I think I made a bit of a fool of myself.'

'No, not at all. But I could see you were worried. It's your father and that young girl, isn't it?'

'Yes. I realise I made that obvious. But it's not sex I'm worried about – more that people will assume it is... And there are other things. Charlie tells me that she's a girl from the drama stream at Westowram High. She's also the leader or one of the leaders of this little group of children going round the village and making people's lives a misery. She targets outsiders who have moved here. She's immensely talented though, Charlie says. Her name is Anne Michaels.'

'I think I know the parents,' Alison said. Of course the Carlsons knew everyone in Slepton.

'Oh? What are they like?'

'Perfectly nice people... Not awfully bright.'

'Well, that's a pity. It'll make it difficult for them to cope. How can dim parents have a child like that?'

'Oh, don't let's get on to heredity. Do you think Chris talking to them might help?'

'Talking to my father might be more to the purpose, but he doesn't respond to reason, or even sympathy... And doesn't Chris usually leave it to the person who is worried or uncertain to approach *him?*'

'That's the idea. And informally. Just to sit down somewhere, anywhere, have a chat, throw suggestions around. Chris loves it all. It's part of the process of healing. You sounded doubtful. Do you think your father would be unlikely to make an approach?'

'I think hell would freeze over first.'

'You hate your father, don't you?'

The suggestion came out of the blue, put very matter-of-factly. She was forced to think it over.

'I think I'd prefer the word "detest".'

'Whatever. I'd understood you did.'

'Well, I've certainly never made any secret of it, but only when I'm with friends.'

'No, you haven't, but it was only last night that I actually felt it. Saw you walking towards him and that girl and saw the body language. Whatever word you prefer to use, you can't stand him.'

'Is that so surprising or unusual? Dreadful people don't lack the power to have children. And if they do, they are likely to be loathed by them. I think too that I looked at that girl and – whatever she's done – I thought: I could have been that girl. I could have been the person that he uses as his acolyte, his worshipper. And I wanted to save her from that.'

'Anyway, I've said what I wanted to say, so I won't drop in. But if you ever want to talk...'

Felicity thought as she put the phone down that Alison was beginning to sound like Chris, to take on the role of universal counsellor and comforter. Or perhaps she just wanted to take over the women. Could it be that she had begun to feel jealous? Felicity liked Alison, but she wasn't sure she had Chris's appeal as someone to be confided in. Chris had a strange way of making himself disappear like the Cheshire cat, and taking on some part of the person who was confiding in him. He became their better self, and could influence their thinking by seeming to come from within them. Alison, more determined and definite, more *human* in fact, did not have that ability, or that appearance of general tolerance that made Chris so approachable.

Charlie was due back about three, but mid-morning Felicity found she was out of milk, wrapped Carola up against the bright, cold weather and walked with her, at her pace, down to the supermarket, which had started opening on a Sunday. It was just outside the door that she was accosted by a couple she didn't know.

'Oh excuse me, but you're Mr Coggenhoe's daughter, aren't you?'

It was the woman who spoke – comfortable, blue-costumed, probably just out of church. The man was vaguer, with a faintly military air that perhaps sprang from his moustache, and a tendency to hang back.

'That's right,' said Felicity, stopping.

'I don't want to take up your time, I'm sure you're busy, with your lovely little girl to look after, but we just wanted to say – because we wouldn't dare to talk to *him* – how much we appreciate your father taking so much trouble with our Anne. It's an honour for her, it really is! To us it's been quite unexpected, and wonderful, because she's been a bit of a handful in the past – until quite recently, actually – and him taking such an interest has really transformed her, hasn't it, Jack?'

'It has that,' said Jack.

'We'd so like it if she could develop the writing side a bit – she's always been interested, but your dad has really brought it out – and we sort of hope that it'll dampen down the drama, which I think was the cause of some of the trouble, not wanting to cast aspersions, but things were happening... So will you tell him we are very grateful – we are, aren't we, Jack?'

'Appreciative.'

'That's it. We appreciate the trouble he's taking. Well, we won't take up any more of your time.'

'I think, you know,' said Felicity as the substantial form started to turn away, 'it would be better if you could tell him yourselves.' She kicked herself the moment it was out. The last thing to help the situation was gushing thanks to her father from fond but imperceptive parents, who in effect would be giving the green light to ... whatever he was aiming to create out of the adolescent clay of Anne Michaels. She felt she had been so anxious to avoid the burden of carrying the naive thanks herself that she had forgotten that her own cool thanks would have been infinitely less dangerous than the Michaelses gush.

'Oh, I don't think we could,' said Mrs Michaels, and gush was what she was doing, even to Felicity. 'We smile if we pass in the streets, and he knows who we are, but no – we couldn't do more. Such a famous novelist, we've heard. It would be months before we could summon up the courage.'

'Well, I'll just mention your appreciation then. Don't let him monopolise Anne though. She'll have her exams to do soon, won't she?'

'Oh yes, next year. But what could be more stimulating for her than an interest taken in her by a great novelist.'

'In the end it's grades people look at on the CV,' said Felicity firmly, and, gathering up Carola in her arms, she went into the little supermarket. Great novelist indeed!

The Price-rite supermarket was humming with customers – ones just out of church, ones on the way to the pub, and ones who had discovered a lack in the middle of cooking the traditional Sunday lunch. To the surprise of some of its more conservative citizens Sunday shopping had quickly become a matter of routine in Slepton Edge, and not at all a cause for shame. Convenience had won its usual victory over principle.

'I saw you talking to the Michaelses,' came a voice from behind Felicity's shoulder. Turning she saw Nancy Stoppard.

'That's right. They introduced themselves.'

Nancy's voice went very low.

'They're rather dim, I'm afraid.'

'Not the brightest lights in the candelabrum,' said Felicity.

'But you mustn't assume they auto-matically get everything wrong,' said Nancy, apparently keen to defend villagers from outsiders. 'They are Anne's parents. They know her best.'

'How did you know we were talking about Anne?'

'What else? I was in the back pew last night, and I saw you interrupting your father's tête-à-tête with Anne.'

Felicity grimaced.

'I thought I was just joining it to make a threesome, but she took off immediately.'

'Yes, and that made you suspicious, didn't it? But why should it? Teenagers don't obey any courtesy codes, and didn't even in my day. And they don't particularly welcome older people whom they don't know.'

'That's true enough, though Anne seems to get on particularly well with older people.'

'Have you any reason to think there's any-thing ... not quite right about this relation-ship?'

Felicity looked at her. Nancy seemed to her a straight person, one who was trying to be honest and to force her to look honestly at a complex situation. It also struck her that by now she must know Rupert Coggen-hoe pretty well.

'Not as such, no. In fact, I feel sure there isn't, if what we're talking about is under-age sex.'

'But you don't like him having admirers at all?'

'There's a streak of vanity in my dad,' began Felicity.

'People had noticed,' said Nancy dryly. The two women looked at each other and then laughed.

'All right – a strong streak. He loves admiration, and he would be over the moon if anyone tried to set up a fan club. I think this kind of relationship is bad for him, rather than for her.'

'But why worry about that? He's in his seventies, you have your own life to live, you don't greatly care for each other, so why can't you let him be? If you can't make your own mistakes at his time of life, when can you?'

'Yes, of course. But I hate to think he might make a slave of her as he made one of my mother. She hardly existed, but just revolved about him. And another thing–'

Nancy put her hand up to stop her.

'If you know something I don't know I don't want to hear it. If he's come up here from Devon to make a fresh start, I'd rather it be that as far as I'm concerned.'

And she went off towards the tills, leaving Felicity once again feeling rebuked. Nancy was quite right that a fresh start should be just that, but if only it was! As far as she could see her father was intent on making exactly the same mistake all over again. She was quite willing to leave him to dig his own grave where Slepton was concerned, as he had in Coombe Barton, but there was the girl to consider. What effect was the intimacy (call it that, with no preconceptions what it consisted of) going to have on her, whether it flourished or was stopped? Now she came to think of it, Madge Easton had been non-communicative about the girl in the previous relationship. Had the girl been devastated, left feeling empty and let down? Or had she just picked up the pieces and got on with her life? Somehow Felicity didn't think it was the latter.

Of course this girl seemed different – all too confident and worldly. Had she in fact gone into the relationship with open eyes? Engineered it, quite possibly. Could it be she was intent on making a public fool of the great (in his own estimation) Rupert Coggenhoe?

The more she thought about it the more likely Felicity felt it to be.

'Mummy, why are you always talking about Grandad?' asked Carola as they made for the tills. 'He's not very interesting.'

By the time they had reached home Felicity had decided she was not going to worry about her father. Ever again.

The path to the quarry began where Forsythia Avenue ended. Tarmac gave way to dirt track, and between the trees there was a splendid view over the lower parts of Halifax. Fifty years ago it would be a prospect of smog. Then the inhabitants hardly ever saw the sun. The Clean Air Act had changed all that. Now, on clear days, you could get a sharp view of the town from the path as it wound around the quarry. It was long disused, and trees, gorse and scrub covered the sides of it – some sides a fairly gentle slope that children could climb up, others precipitous and quite non-negotiable whether up or down. It was not a popular walking place, and no fences or railings had been put up along the path, even at the more dangerous spots.

Rupert Coggenhoe sometimes walked here, when the plot of his new book or his life had reached a knotty point. The fact that the Slepton Edgers found it fairly sinister and threatening did not bother him – in fact he did not notice it. Nor did it bother him that he was frequently alone here. On the day after the carol service he left his bungalow in the early afternoon, having had a phone call from Anne Michaels to say she couldn't get round to see him that day. She called from a phone box, and acted up the part of a schoolgirl calling one of her girl-friends. Rupert Coggenhoe knew what she was doing, because she told him. He smiled indulgently. When she rang off she told him she'd come and visit him the next day, after school. Coggenhoe felt warmed by her friendship and her devotion to him. He dwelt on those things as he walked. Oddly he was not an imaginative man except where he himself was concerned, and then he was more concerned to imagine slights than to imagine dangers.

He walked on, seeing no one until he came to one of the more dangerous parts of the footpath, and then it didn't occur to him to wonder why the person he saw was lingering there, rather than walking either towards him or away from him. He went blundering forward regardless.

Charlie finished his early Sunday stretch at three o'clock, and made for his car, parked by the empty Leeds market. It was a bright, cold December afternoon and he had been out for most of Sunday morning bringing bad news and good to people involved in a variety of his cases. Felicity had phoned him while he was wolfing down a Marks and Spencer's sandwich to tell him her new resolution not to worry about her father, and he had had to strain his stomach muscles to prevent himself from laughing. Perhaps that was why she had phoned him at work, though: to cheer him up with something to hoot at. Still, if only halfway serious it was at least a step in the right direction. She knew what she ought to be doing, if she was unlikely to follow her resolution for very long. Her phoning him at work with things that could and should wait was one of the last relics of the uncertainty that had been so strong in her when they had first met, and could be put down to her upbringing with a man like Rupert Coggenhoe in the house.

He was still thinking over the oddity of Felicity's family and how she had escaped them for several years only to be mentally recaptured, when he stopped in the village to buy a packet of cigarettes in the corner shop and was hailed by the genial figure of Desmond Pinkhurst, still apparently on a 'high' from the success of his performance in rehearsal. They stood in the darkening street talking for a second or third time about this when Desmond changed the subject.

'I say, your revered father-in-law isn't getting himself into potential hot water, is he?'

Charlie's heart sank, but he retained his native caution.

'He may be. We certainly hope not.'

'Word to the wise. Tell him to watch his step.'

Charlie shook his head.

'Felicity has already tried to. It's not easy.'

'But it *is* easy to slip into something little by little, and then find yourself up to your neck in it and sinking fast.'

He spoke with apparent feeling.

'Are you speaking from bitter experience, Desmond?'

Desmond smiled sunnily.

'Oh no, dear boy. I think I told you that when it comes to good old-fashioned rumpy-pumpy I'm quite happy to be counted out. But she did offer, dear boy. And I hate to think what would have happened to poor old Desmond if he had taken her up on it.'

'Is it Anne Michaels we are talking about?'

'Who else, dear boy?'

'She offered, did she? Just like that.'

'Well, pretty much so. She was in the Black Heifer with her parents, drinking orange juice which I wouldn't mind betting was spiked from a miniature vodka or some such thing concealed about her burgeoning person. We were all together, laughing and joking – though they're not awfully enter-taining, the Michaelses – and as they were getting up to go, the mother putting on her coat and the father taking glasses back to the bar, this young lady – I use the word as a courtesy title – stood over me, put her mouth close to my ear, and said: "If you ever want a quick poke with something young and fresh come along to me and we can come to some arrangement".'

'Good Lord,' said Charlie. 'What did you do?'

'I wasn't called upon to do anything but

splutter because the father came back. I probably would have said that Vi Varley, the landlady of the Heifer, was more my idea of young and fresh than she was, and she's had most of the men in the village over the last twenty years. Luckily I didn't have to, because you should always deal with the young with kid gloves. But I saw her a week or so later in the supermarket and I put *my* mouth close to *her* ear and I whispered "Not on your life". And I didn't use my sibilant whisper that I developed for Kenneth Williams-type roles, but kept it genuinely quiet. She probably thought I would find the offer flattering, but I didn't.'

'Frightening rather, I'd have thought.'

'Absolutely right, old boy! Bang on target! Anyone who took her up on her offer would be absolutely in her power.'

Charlie told Felicity about Desmond's revelation when they had a moment together (actually nearly half an hour) while Carola was on her mother's mobile to a school-friend. Charlie had thought it was a wonderful sign of precocity when his daughter mastered a mobile. Now he worried that it would shorten her childhood, but it did keep her amused for long periods. As her mother's telephone bill testified.

'So according to Desmond, Anne Michaels was offering herself to an older man, and one with some kind of a reputation beyond the village.'

Felicity was very worried, but thought before she replied.

'If there *was* anything sexual between her and Dad, and it came to court, Desmond's evidence would be important, wouldn't it?'

'Yes, it would. In the past juries were apt to assume that the older man was the guilty party and the initiator of the affair. Scales have fallen from their eyes in recent years, though there might be a charge of statutory rape, due to her age.'

'I suppose there's no proof that the offer was seriously intended, is there?'

'No. That kind of proof is difficult. The best thing would be if she could be shown to have had or be having a relationship of a similar sexual kind with someone else.'

'Not Desmond, anyway.'

'No, I believe him absolutely. But there are other candidates. She is Harvey Buck-worth's favourite young actress. And any of her other teachers could have the hots for her.'

'That's a horrible expression.'

'Sorry. It's these Australian soaps. Anyway, there's another danger: even if the advance to Desmond was *not* a serious offer, one could well imagine that a fifteen-year-old, very sexually aware, if she had had a knock-back after making advances to your father–'

'And I do still think that was the way it would have happened.'

'–might well invent an affair to get attention, to get revenge, just to create mayhem.'

'I have wondered about that,' Felicity admitted. 'This seems *more* dangerous than the one in Coombe Barton because this girl is not a sad, lonely creature but a born trouble-maker – witness her poisonous little gang.'

They were interrupted by a ring from the immobile telephone.

'Carola, put a sock in it, you've had long enough,' yelled Charlie.

'Oh, do I have to?' protested Carola, but she rang off.

'352076,' said Charlie.

'Charlie. It's Ben.'

'Ben? Ben Costello?'

It seemed presumptuous to Charlie that they were already on Christian name terms.

'That's right. Has your father-in-law been round today?'

'Today? No. I don't think we're in his good books.'

'Have you been round to his?'

'No. I was on duty from seven until three, but Felicity said she hadn't seen him since last night.' A cold feeling was rising inside him, so he asked outright: 'What is this?'

'We've just had a report. A walker has found a body in the quarry at Beacon Falls. She says it is Rupert Coggenhoe. That is your father-in-law, isn't it?'

'Yes. Oh my God. Shall we come out?'

'No. We'll come and get you if identification is needed. It could be some big mistake. Stay there. I'll keep in touch.'

Charlie, as he put the phone down and turned to Felicity, noted the time on the dining room clock. Four forty-five. It was a policeman's reaction. But it was quite wasted now. This wasn't his case at all. If it wasn't an accident, which he felt in his bones it was not, or a suicide, which he felt it couldn't be, he was going to be part of this case from a quite unaccustomed side of the fence.

8

Wondering

The police came to take Felicity to identify the body at five-thirty. Charlie tried to insist on coming with her.

'No. This is something I have to do on my own.'

Charlie knew the expression of obstinacy on her face.

'You sound like John Wayne,' he protested.

'I just mean that I have to make a last

farewell, without apology or regret.'

So Charlie stayed at home and looked after Carola. Felicity had already told her that Grandad was dead, and she would never be seeing him again. She was definitely interested and definitely pleased. Her reactions were more naked than her parents', but not essentially different. When Charlie said he thought there would be a church service, she looked as if she was planning to be a tree fairy.

At a quarter to six there was a knock on the door and Chris Carlson put his head round it.

'Tell me to go away if you'd rather,' he said.

'Not at all. Come on in.' Charlie gestured him to a seat. 'Carola is having a rare session with her doll.'

Chris sank into the armchair.

'I didn't want you to think I was one of those ghouls who go around seeking out places of sickness or bereavement.'

'Chris, why would I think that? You know you're a friend. How did you find out?'

'From Nancy Stoppard. But it's all round the village.'

'I suppose it was bound to be. Felicity's gone to identify the body. She wanted to be alone.'

'People identifying the bodies of near ones often do.'

Charlie shook his head.

'I know you're choosing your words carefully, Chris, but it won't do. He wasn't "near" any more than he was "loved". That's what I think she wants to come to terms with. Then she'll put him behind her and get on with her life – *our* lives. If we're allowed to.'

'Why shouldn't you be?'

Charlie shrugged.

'I don't know. But after the affair at Coombe Barton I just got the idea that it had to be–' He pulled himself up. He was being unpolicemanly. 'I can't believe he'd commit suicide. And why should it be an accident? He was perfectly steady on his pins.'

'Now you are being melodramatic,' said Chris. 'Why *shouldn't* it be an accident – maybe a heart attack as he was walking too close to the edge?'

'I suppose that's a possibility. But why walk close to the edge? I've been around the quarry. The path is a couple of feet from the edge. Come to that, why walk there at all on a cold December afternoon?'

'Wasn't your pa-in-law a walker?'

'I don't really know. I hardly know him at all, and his habits I know almost nothing about. Perhaps he went for walks when he had trouble with his plots. Felicity will know. *Perhaps* Felicity will know. Her knowledge is rather out of date.'

Chris leaned back in the chair and looked

straight at him.

'Charlie, I know you're having doubts about me – about what I do, whether it's useful, my motives–'

'Chris, you're exaggerating! Getting paranoid.'

'Maybe, but I don't think so. You know, I do sometimes help, do sometimes give people confidence to do something they deep down want to do. I mean something brave, like Desmond is doing. Or it might be the moral courage to avoid doing something that would bring unhappiness to them or someone near them. Anyone could do it – it's just a question of listening warmly and sympathetically. But it's something I like doing, and that people seem to want me to do.'

Something about that little speech worried Charlie, without his being quite clear in his mind what it was.

'Chris, are you trying to tell me something?' Charlie saw at once that his question made Chris feel slightly sheepish. 'Have you been talking to the late Rupert, giving him advice perhaps?'

'Well ... no, *not* giving him advice. He didn't ask for it, and frankly I can't imagine him ever actually asking for it. I don't shower people with moral guidance out of the blue.'

'No, I can't see him asking for advice either. He was too confident in himself and his own judgment. So what happened?'

Chris sighed. He was obviously getting the feeling of being in the witness box and suffering cross-examination.

'It was earlier today in the Black Heifer, and it was just after opening, twelve o'clock with not many people there because church was not finished, and he and I began talking at the bar.'

'How often had you talked to him before?'

'Hardly ever. At most twice. Once was about Carola and the impending birth of his grandchild, and he didn't have much to say on them.'

'I bet he didn't.'

'Anyway, this time he began talking about himself, and how the planning of his next book was going. It apparently was more realistic than usual, a modern tale full of real people of today was how he described it. Then he began talking about having an "inspiration". Well, after a time I realised that he wasn't talking about a wonderful idea, but about a human inspiration.'

'Oh my God,' groaned Charlie. 'Did he give a name?'

'No, he didn't. But you'd told me about the problems back in Coombe Barton, and I'd seen him with the Michaels girl at the carol service, so I thought about Dickens and Ibsen and writers like that and the part younger women – girls, almost – played in their later lives and writings. And that made me a bit uneasy. It's a relationship fraught with difficulties and potential for nasty comment and prejudice in a small place like Slepton Edge. And as often as not it's quite innocent – just a sentimental attachment, a piece of nostalgia about youth, its enthusiasm and purity – that kind of thing.'

'Felicity is convinced that's what it is – was – in her father's case.'

Chris nodded.

'She's probably right. But the danger is when that's not how it's seen by the people around. And that can have consequences both for the older person and the younger one.'

'And so you warned him?'

Chris looked uneasy again.

'Not to say warned. Just tried to make him aware of the downside.'

Charlie was not inclined to give up on the inquisition.

'What exactly did you say?'

Chris sighed, and thought.

'I said: "That's wonderful for you, and for her too. But be careful people here don't start talking about it. It's always bad for children when they are talked about".'

'So what did he say?'

'He said: "Not her. She loves being talked about. And she's not a child."'

They looked at each other.

'Did he mean by that,' asked Charlie

slowly, feeling his way, 'that he was talking about a grown woman, not Anne Michaels? Or that Anne was very mature for her age?'

'I don't know. He walked off at that point – or stalked, I should say. But I took it to mean that Anne was in all important ways a grown-up woman. And that he didn't at all care for my interference.'

Charlie groaned.

Ben Costello grasped Felicity's arm and led her into the mortuary. They turned towards the far wall, and to a stone slab with a body on it. Felicity's heart thumped when she recognised the old green sports jacket. It had been bought long ago in an outfitter's in Exeter that catered for the gentry. It had been old-fashioned then, and now looked antiquated. She had still been spending university vacations at home when he bought it. Recently she'd seen him wearing it to do some desultory gardening – clearing up twigs and dead leaves. He'd hate being exposed on a mortuary slab in shabby old gardening clothes. Unless he'd caught on that the gentry rather specialised in dressing shabbily.

They came closer to the body inside the clothes.

'Yes, that's him,' Felicity said.

She tried to take in the detail, the tear on the shoulder of the jacket, the dirt on the grey flannel trousers and the shoes, the sandy-coloured smear across the left cheek. She must have a picture of him in her mind, to tell Charlie about later. She shuffled off Ben Costello's hand and went closer. The half of her mind that believed in God was trying to frame a prayer. It came out as one that all his sins should be forgiven him. The sceptical side of her mind suggested this was a tall order.

She turned and walked back to the door, Costello following behind her. Outside she looked at him questioningly.

'Would you like me to get someone to drive you home?' he asked. 'Or would you be willing to answer a few questions now?'

Felicity thought. She felt exhausted and yet excited. She felt ashamed of the latter emotion, but she could not deny it. She was now free, she was entirely her own person. Her own – and Charlie's, Carola's and Little Foetus's. She was her own world, un-shadowed by the past. She need feel no guilt, no resentment. Charlie was at home looking after Carola. He wasn't going any-where. She wanted to get it over.

'Questions, please,' she said.

'Good girl,' said Costello, approvingly if unfashionably. Felicity let herself be led to a room on the second floor. It was all very informal, with no suggestion that she was under suspicion. She thought with surprise that there had been no suggestion that there was anything to be suspicious about.

'Now,' said Ben Costello, 'let's be clear from the outset – or maybe I should say unclear. Because we have no idea at the moment whether what we are talking about is an accident, suicide, manslaughter or murder. So all I am doing now is trying to make the situation and background clearer.' Felicity nodded. 'Now, did you see or talk to your father earlier today?'

'No. Neither.'

'When did you last see or talk to him?'

'Last night at the carol service.' She added, still embarrassed by the memories, 'The encounter you saw.'

'When you interrupted your father and Anne Michaels?'

Felicity grimaced.

'I didn't mean to interrupt. I meant to join.' She heard the bitterness in her tone and said: 'Sorry. I know you all saw, and drew your own conclusions. It would have been much better if I'd left them alone. You all probably thought there was something going on between my poor old father and this young chick. In point of fact I don't believe that for a moment. But I made sure everyone else did. Just what we didn't want.'

'Surely what you didn't want was for your father to get entangled in that way in the first place?'

'True. But just as bad is *not* to be entangled, but to be gossiped about as if you were.'

'And that had happened in the past to your father?'

Felicity took a deep breath, and decided to come clean. 'Why not? He was dead, and about to become part of her past.

'I think so. I mean I *know* there was gossip, but I think it was untrue. But that's why he suddenly plonked himself on us here in Yorkshire. It happened where he was living before, in Coombe Barton, in Devon. Pretty little cottage, hollyhocks in the garden, roses climbing round the door.'

'Sounds idyllic,' said Ben Costello. Why leave that to come to Yorkshire – except to be near you, of course.'

'That was the least of his reasons. There was a snake in the Eden, and he introduced it himself.'

And she told him, briefly, the gist of what had happened in Coombe Barton: his using Dora Catchpole when the other lady-slaves started melting away, and his attachment to himself of the woman's grandchild Kylie. Costello looked sceptical.

'Sounds innocent, if unwise.'

'That's about the limit of it, if I'm reading the rune right. But you can see why it would cause a fuss in a little community. First of all the women rallied round after my mother's death, but they soon found out that he was

136

an exploiter – it's the sort of relationship he understands best. Under*stood*. And the thought must have occurred to them when he took up with this schoolgirl that the exploitative nature of the man could extend beyond what they'd offered him – work, services and so on – to a sexual exploitation, if he was interested in that way in young girls. And then the parents came into the picture, the whole family in fact, and the gossip mill started to turn speculation into fact. It's how the tabloid newspapers operate on a national level. Gossip does the same on the local level.'

Costello nodded, his dark eyes becoming calculating.

'And was the same thing happening in Slepton Edge?'

'I don't know. I don't think so – or rather, it was in the earliest stages, with the women who had helped him settle in falling away as they saw they got no gratitude or genuine friendship. But the process had hardly started, and that's why I kicked myself over what happened last night. I practically announced my suspicions to the whole village by going to break up their conversation. Or so people must have thought.'

'It wasn't quite that–'

'But I could see speculation in all of your eyes, you who were watching. And the truth is, I didn't have any suspicions of my dad –

not on the sexual level. But I was afraid that he'd use his little fame to tie the girl to him, get a willing disciple, and I saw that that could have consequences nearly as disastrous as a May-December sexual relationship would have.'

'She looked to me a very self-possessed and modern young lady.'

'She is – at fifteen! And she's a budding actress in the drama stream at Westowram High. Quite brilliant, Charlie says. And she has a little gang of younger children who go round targeting newcomers to the village – or that seems to be what they're doing.'

'Yes – Harridance has told me about that, your husband's contact. But what are you saying about the girl's motives?'

Felicity thought hard before replying.

'That she could have been entering into this relationship – *luring* Dad into it – with destructive intentions: blackmail, or perhaps just making his reputation in the village so bad that he was forced out. Or maybe just destroying him as a person for the fun of it. That little gang of children suggests she likes power, rejoices in it, just any manifestation of it.'

Costello shifted uneasily in his chair, but he conceded: 'I could imagine she's pretty hot to handle. Difficult for the parents.'

'I was thanked by them this morning because, they said, Dad was making a change for the better in their daughter by encouraging her literary ambitions. The wilder side, they thought, was encouraged by the drama interest, presumably bringing out the exhibitionist streak in her. Nancy Stoppard said she thought parents understood their children best. In this case I rather doubt it.'

'Though to be fair, they could be right about the drama.' Ben Costello sat back in his chair and thought. 'All this is very interesting, but only if there's more to your dad's death than meets the eye.'

Felicity nodded.

'And what meets the eye, do you think?' she asked.

'An accidental fall during a walk on his own when his mind was occupied – with his latest book, perhaps, or with his lovely young disciple.'

'It's possible. So is a heart attack.'

Costello leant forward, now all energy.

'But you assumed, as soon as you heard of your father's body in the quarry that it was – well, at least that there was something suspicious about it.'

'How do you know that?'

'The whole direction of this conversation.'

Felicity thought for a while without answering.

'I suppose I did,' she said at last. 'Yes, I definitely did. And now I come to think of it, it *is* rather absurd, to assume that about a man in his early seventies. I think it must be the combination of learning about the events back in Coombe Barton, seeing something similar perhaps starting here, and then the sudden shock of the death. And there was also the fact that my father was a very dislikable man. Not spectacularly awful, like Evelyn Waugh, but still deeply unpleasant because he was so self-obsessed, manipulative, unfeeling.'

'You really disliked your father?'

'Yes.'

'Did Charlie dislike him too?'

'Charlie can speak for himself.'

'Of course. But I'd like to hear your opinion.'

'In a different way I suppose you could say he disliked him, though it's much less personal with him. He disliked him for what he did to me. I was a very mixed-up kid when Charlie first knew me. But until recently Charlie barely knew him. Intense exposure to him on three or four family occasions – that had been the limit of it.'

'You're being very honest with me.'

'Charlie is a policeman. He really believes that being honest with the police saves a lot of time and trouble.'

'Good for him. Pity he can't have anything to do with this investigation, if there turns out to be anything to investigate, which frankly I doubt.'

'Of course if that does turn out to be the case he'll be completely honest with you. And in any case we've nothing to hide.'

'Oh, everyone has something to hide,' said Costello cheerfully.

'Anyway,' said Charlie to Chris, still sitting in the living room chair, 'you did as much as you could be expected to do to warn poor old Rupert in your first real talk to him. I doubt if you'd have got through to him even if you'd talked to him a lot. Quite apart from anything else, I think he'd have run a mile from being classed with Desmond Pinkhurst and all the others who come to you for advice.'

'If he even noticed that they did,' said Chris.

'Oh, I think he would have. The thing about egotistical people is not that they don't notice things, it's that everything they notice is transformed in their own minds into how it affects *them*, or contrasts with them, or is of use to them. Rupert would not have wanted to be thought in need of advice. If he had any problems he was the one who could solve them. And he was, in his own mind, the great novelist who saw and understood everything.'

'Anyway, I'm glad you don't think anything I said could have affected what happened.'

'How could it have? Do you imagine

Rupert was so worried by the possibilities that you had spelled out that he wandered off the path and over the edge?'

Chris looked sheepish again.

'Put like that it does sound daft.'

'Set your mind at rest. It's not something that needs even mentioning. There won't be any record of disastrous advice given by you should you decide to run for mayor.'

Chris stood up at once and looked hard at Charlie.

'Why do you mention that? I told you, I haven't decided yet.'

'Not consciously. But I think you will.'

'And you disapprove.'

It wasn't a question, but Charlie answered it as one.

'No, I don't. But I just can't see why you should want to do a non-job like that. Not if you weigh it against going back into medicine in some shape or form.'

'But it doesn't have to be a non-job,' protested Chris. 'It can be made into something really useful, and close to ordinary people. They could be encouraged to come direct to the Mayor's office with their difficulties, and know they'd speak to me or to someone who really understood whatever it was that they were het up about.'

Charlie raised his eyebrows.

'Chris, if you got in, you'd have the apparatus of all the three main political parties against you. You'd be even more of a cipher than if you were a political nominee.'

'I don't agree. You're being much too negative.'

'I want to see you being *really* useful. You're in danger of deceiving yourself. The problem is that you are coming to regard yourself as indispensable, whereas what you really are is an optional extra.'

Chris laughed, but there was unease in the laughter. When he took his leave a few minutes later Charlie regretted having hurt him. Really he liked and admired Chris more than almost anyone he'd met. He was so fresh and open and unafraid. On the man-to-man level he was warm, humorous, sympathetic and useful. Was the human level, Charlie wondered, what Chris had not found in his work as a consultant?

He had complained about patients being railroaded through the system, and in any case these days medicine was a matter of science, not of a close relationship between doctor and patient. That seemed to be the philosophy of all the recent governments, anyway. This new function he had taken on as advisor, comforter, shoulder to cry on, gave him all the human contact he had lacked when working on the conveyor belt of his old job. But it's not the sort of human contact I'd want a lot of, thought Charlie.

And Chris was indeed very sharp. He had

seen that Charlie was beginning to have doubts about him almost before he was aware of it himself. But the doubts he had were not really about Chris as a person, only fears that he was taking a wrong course – one that would prolong his absence from the medical world.

Felicity came home before he had a chance to get his thoughts in order. She told him about her identification of the body, her interview with Ben Costello and her thoughts on her father's death. She shed a few tears.

'They're tears for *me*,' she said fiercely, 'not for him. I'm sorry for myself because I didn't have the dad that so many girls seem to have – warm, supportive, lovable. It's sheer self-pity.'

She told him that Costello had emphasised he could have nothing to do with the investigation.

'Of *course* I know that,' said Charlie, exasperated. 'Does he think I'm a complete airhead? Or that you know nothing, in spite of your being a policeman's wife?'

'I expect he'll be glad to have an important case all to himself if it turns out to be a case at all.'

'I don't doubt he will,' said Charlie. 'Any policeman would. But there's nothing in police regulations to stop me talking to people.'

9

Getting Somewhere

Monday was one of two days in the week when Felicity taught in the English Department of Leeds University. It was this work that subsidised her attempts to write the Great Modern English Novel. Charlie was not in the least surprised when, the day after her father's death, she got up and breakfasted early and showed all the usual signs of being about to drive to Headingley. It was all of a piece with refusing to regard herself as bereaved or bereft. Life had already reverted to business as usual, because she felt as usual. She picked up her books, kissed Charlie, and then went out to the car. Charlie, who had the day off after his Sunday stint of duty, pottered around the kitchen and prepared to take Carola off to nursery school.

But he was surprised when at twenty to nine, there was a knock at the door. Who did he know who called at that hour? His surprise was not lessened when he opened the door and saw Harvey Buckworth waiting rather awkwardly on the step. The teacher's nondescript but well-intentioned face was creased with frowns of concern.

'I say, I'm sorry to trouble you. I heard of your loss, and I just wanted to say, well...' He faded away, artistically.

'It's been a big shock,' said Charlie, choosing his words with care.

'It must have been. I'm afraid I haven't read any of his books, but I'll make the effort now. I suppose there will be an obituary in *The Times* that will tell me which are the best ones.'

'Maybe,' said Charlie, scepticism written all over his face. 'Probably one of their short obituaries all bundled together with other ones. Whatever they may say in Slepton Edge he wasn't particularly well-known or particularly good.'

'Really?... I say, I wonder if I could come in for a moment.'

'Yes,' said Charlie, looking round at his daughter and her mess. 'Don't mind Carola. She won't take down your words and use them in evidence against you. I assume this is private.'

'Well ... delicate, you might say. Something I wouldn't want to go beyond these four walls.'

He wielded a powerful cliché, Charlie thought, for one who was apparently of an artistic nature.

'Sit down,' he said. 'Come clean. Tell me all. I'm not a part of the investigation, by the way, for obvious reasons.'

'Investigation? Oh, I suppose there has to be one, doesn't there?'

It was odd. He looked terrified.

'Well, any sudden, unexplained death needs to be looked into. There's nothing particularly frightening in the word "investigation".' He waited. Harvey Buckworth gave the impression that he was internally squirming, but he said nothing. Charlie suppressed strong feelings of irritation. 'Well, come on.'

'Come on?'

'You said this was some kind of delicate matter.'

'Yes, of course... Well, it's the drama stream... I told you it was under threat ... that a lot of people don't like what we're doing at Westowram High.'

'Yes, you did.'

'Well, I wanted to ask you, when you're questioned, to keep the drama students out if it. Don't mention that you've been to see them, don't mention you gave them a warning, don't mention the plays we're doing, or any of the children who are pupils in the stream.'

Charlie sat for a moment, meditating. So much for the feigned surprise at the word 'investigation'. He'd come specifically to ask for his prize piglets to be kept out of the show. But why should he have thought they would be in it? Apart, perhaps, from one.

'I came along to see your child stars because of an incident of harassment. I also came quite unofficially. Do you know of any connection between the harassment and the death of my father-in-law?'

'No, no … of course not.'

'Then it's difficult to see why you came to talk to me. Unless you're worried about your Miranda.'

'My–? Oh yes, well…'

'Is there talk around the town? Or were you at the carol service?'

'Well, actually both. There was bound to be talk, with a death like that. Nobody has fallen into the quarry for years, except one old woman who had cancer. And the carol service is not really my thing, but I'd trained the Christmas fairies, so–'

'So you saw my father-in-law and Anne Michaels.'

'Yes. And I live a little bit further down the hill, so I'd seen you and your wife coming and going, and I thought–'

'Tell me, was the carol service the first you knew of the connection with Anne?'

'Yes. Oh yes, absolutely the first. Look it's nearly nine. I've got a class in twenty minutes. I just – well, I hope you'll keep what I said in mind.'

'Oh, I'll keep it in mind,' said Charlie.

Parading slowly through the streets of

Slepton on the way to the nursery school, with Carola seriously surveying the parents and children while clutching his hand, Charlie thought over the talk with Harvey Buckworth. He was, clearly, afraid that the threat to his drama stream in Westowram High would be aggravated by the death of Rupert Coggenhoe. The connection of his star female player with the elderly author would do him no good in a tight, prim little community such as Slepton Edge, and might even – the Michaelses being obviously dubious already about the drama classes – result in the loss of his Miranda. Still, Anne's connection with Rupert was encouraged by them, and was not to be attributed to any school interference. And there was no reason, except the exaggerations and hysteria of local gossip, for Harvey to see Rupert's death as anything but an accident. Or was there?

Why did he get the idea that Anne Michaels wasn't the only cause of Harvey Buckworth's evident concern?

Charlie was well enough known at the nursery school to be greeted by many of the parents, some of whom followed up with 'I *was* sorry to hear–' 'Tell Felicity we were shocked to hear–' and 'I've always said there should be a fence up there'. He fended off sympathy as well as he knew how, but he was finding that being hypocritical about an unloved parent was not easy. He knew it was even more difficult for Felicity, and thought most of the sympathisers suspected how relations stood between father and daughter. Carola was just running joyfully into the building when Charlie, turning to leave the play area, saw a face that he recognised. It was a boy, leading a much younger girl by the hand. After a second or two of brain-racking he realised it was the black boy who had played Trinculo in the scenes from *The Tempest*. He went up to him, smiling recognition.

'Hello. I don't think I was told your name.'

'Dwayne. Dwayne Vickery.'

'Not at school today then?'

'No. Mum thought I'd better not go... I'm not feeling too good. Sore throat.'

There was no sign of hoarseness, though. There was an embarrassment about the boy that puzzled Charlie.

'Are you sure that was why your mother didn't want you to go to school?' he asked.

'Sore throat, like I said. I gotta go. They're going in. Goodbye.' And the boy scurried towards the building and safety. Thoughtful – in fact speculative – Charlie walked towards home, hoping that the boy would be collecting his sister in three hours' time.

When he got back home the light on his answer-machine was flashing, and he pressed 'Play'.

'Hello, Charlie. It's Ben Costello at the Halifax Station. Any chance of you coming down and having a routine chat? No sign of a report from the post-mortem yet, I'm afraid.'

After a moment's thought Charlie phoned the duty sergeant at Halifax, who turned out to be his friend Peter Harridance, to give the message to Costello that he was on his way.

He didn't have time to swap words with Harridance because Ben Costello was waiting by the desk to lead him through to one of the more informal interview rooms such as Felicity had been taken to the night before. 'Just a chat to put me in the picture,' said Ben, and they both sat in chairs that were some way between upright and easy.

'You'll have an idea of what Mrs Peace told me last night, I expect,' Costello began. 'The broad outline, anyway. I don't know if there's anything you want to add?'

Charlie thought long and hard.

'Felicity's the expert. Long exposure through childhood and adolescence until she made her escape. The weeks since we all came to Slepton have been my first long exposure to her father. Speaking as a virtual outsider I would just say I found him antipathetic.'

'Any particular reason?'

'His complete egotism. The fact that he used people all the time.' He thought, then

151

decided to be honest. 'Little things, like his complete lack of interest in Carola and the one on the way. The fact that when it was suggested that he might be sending Chrismas cards to the women who'd helped him over his bereavement in Coombe Barton he acted as if he'd be doing them a big favour if he did it at all. He expected everything to be done for him, and refused to give anything in return.'

'Had this resulted in any blow-ups?'

'No,' said Charlie, rather surprised now he thought about it. 'I'm glad about that now, because we don't have to have any guilt feelings. But if he'd lived it would only have been a matter of time.'

'I had the feeling that a blow-up was brewing at the carol service.'

'Ah yes, that. We saw how it must have looked. Felicity was worried there was going to be a replay of Coombe Barton. I gather she's told you all about that.'

'Pretty much all.'

'If I may make a suggestion–'

'Can't you talk fucking English?' exploded Costello. '"If I may make a suggestion". You sound like a fucking Bishop... Sorry.'

Charlie's eyes narrowed, but he maintained his ostentatious cool.

'No, I'm sorry. I expect it comes from being married to an English graduate steeped in nineteenth-century novels.'

'No, it's me should be apologising. I've only had three hours' sleep.'

'Anyway I was going to suggest that Felicity has made a bit too much of Coombe Barton in her own mind. It may have been the sort of little local brouhaha that would have died down in a few weeks because there was really nothing in it.'

'Maybe,' said Costello. 'I said "pretty much all". It occurred to me after your wife had gone that she didn't tell me how her father and Anne Michaels came together. Where, how did they meet?'

Charlie's forehead creased.

'Do you know, I hadn't thought of that. Felicity and I haven't talked about it, so I don't suppose she has either. Search me. I know it wasn't like Coombe Barton, where the relationship sprang up when one of the women who acted as one of his unpaid servants brought her granddaughter up with her one day and it went on from there. The Michaelses apparently hadn't met Rupert, and they told Felicity when she met them accidentally at the supermarket that they wouldn't dare approach "the great author" to thank him for what he was doing for Anne – turning her away from drama and towards writing, or so they thought. I don't know the Michaels family and it may be worth your while checking up on them.'

'I will.'

'Could Rupert have had anything to do with the drama stream at Westowram High? It's possible, though I think he would have told us if he had. Anything that ministered to his sense of being a person of importance was passed on to all and sundry.'

'And your wife told me that Anne Michaels was part of the little gang that made life difficult for newcomers to the area?'

'She was the leader. Haven't heard much of them recently. Coggenhoe was a new-comer, of course, but it seems a pretty unlikely way of getting acquainted.'

'I'm inclined to your wife's view that there was nothing sexual going on with this Michaels girl. She seems to come into the picture under too many separate hats: actress, gang leader, possibly abused child. I rather think she's going to turn out to be a red herring.'

'Maybe.'

'Had there been much talk about this possible affair?'

'Very little, if any. Felicity admits that if there was a chance of this turning into a rerun of the Coombe Barton affair, it was in its early stages. The parents were entirely happy with things, flattered even, delighted, as I say, to have her mind taken off acting, which they saw as the root cause of some recent problems... On the other hand Chris Carlson tried to give Rupert a warning about possible talk, damage to the girl and so on, and Rupert simply slapped him down.'

'I see. I must ask him about that if anything suspicious is found in the post-mortem. At the moment we're all in the air, and probably wasting our time. Getting more general, I'm not a literary type so tell me: was your father-in-law an important writer?'

'No. He'd just written a lot.'

'Is that your wife speaking?'

'Probably most of my views on Coggenhoe are a replay of Felicity's views. You need to keep an open mind. But yes, she's the literary one, and the reason I speak like I do sometimes.' Costello nodded, not seeming to be embarrassed though. 'I've read one or two of the books, and found them difficult to get through. She says he writes a lot of different kinds of books – romance, historical, crime and so on – but is never top-notch in any one of them. So if you went into Halifax Library you'd probably find they had a lot of his books but he's never become well-known, never a "name", because he spreads a meagre talent pretty thin. The lack of big success really riled him. Felicity said he never could realise that he was writing "popular" fiction: in his own mind he was a quality writer.'

'Your wife is not exactly unbiased.'

Charlie shrugged, trying not to show irritation.

'Aren't we all, about our parents? One way

or another. Felicity is sharp, and she's not likely to deceive herself.'

'Maybe. But you agree her feelings about her father are pretty strong?'

'She saw him as turning her mother into a mindless drudge, and trying to do the same to her. By the way, is there any indication of the time Rupert went over the edge?'

'Not yet. Some time before five o'clock, when he was found. Why?'

'I thought I might give Felicity an alibi.'

'For what it's worth. But she's not a suspect,' Costello went on hurriedly, seeing he'd gone too far. 'Nobody is a suspect, as long as there's no evidence of a crime.'

Charlie bit back all sorts of reply.

'Well, for the record I was home by four o'clock, and she and Carola were there then.'

'I'll bear it in mind. You do realise, don't you Charlie, that you can have nothing at all to do with this enquiry.'

Charlie did not care for being treated as an idiot. His voice rose higher.

'Of *course* I know I can't play any part in it.'

'Don't get on your high horse. I'm just wanting it quite clear from the word Go: if there is anything to look into this will be my case, maybe with a senior officer from this station above me. If there is nothing, then of course there's no problem.'

'Agreed,' said Charlie, but he felt there was a problem, and it was called Costello. 'By the way, what if there's uncertainty whether he was or was not pushed? Medical evidence in a case like this can point both ways.'

'I hadn't thought of that. Murder hasn't often come my way.'

'How do you distinguish a shove from all the injuries the body will have incurred when falling down the quarry side? It's a bold doctor who will be categorical in that sort of case.'

'I'll bear that in mind. Now, let's just sum up our little talk and we'll both get on our ways. Rupert Coggenhoe's circle of acquaintances since he came to live in Slepton Edge would be, as far as you know, yourselves, Anne Michaels, and the women who took care of some of the daily practicalities for him. How the Michaels acquaintanceship started up we don't know, or what it amounted to.'

'No. By the way I forgot to mention: according to Chris Carlson he was starting to refer to Anne as his "inspiration".'

'Christ.'

'Exactly.'

'Anybody else in the picture, Charlie?'

'Hmmm. Casual pals in the Black Heifer – male ones there, mostly. He usually had a few words with the landlord, he'd had one or two short chats with Chris, and some with Desmond Pinkhurst, though I think he didn't hit it off with him. I wonder about the schoolteachers. Schools like to have an author around now and then to talk to the kids.'

'Schoolteachers, you say. One would be Harvey Buckworth I imagine. Who else?'

'There's a chap who was made a victim by the children in the drama stream – name of Warburton. I don't know him myself, but I know he lives in Slepton, or nearby.'

'We mustn't get obsessed by the children. Anne Michaels is the only connection with them so far as we know.'

'Fair enough.'

'We'd better get along,' said Ben Costello, standing up. 'I've got a lot on my plate. Thanks for your help.'

'If anything occurs to me that I've forgotten I'll let you know.'

They walked down the corridor and stairs and into the outer office, which was empty except for Sergeant Harridance, on duty there.

'Hello Peter. You know Charlie Peace don't you? He's the coming man in Leeds. Stick to him and you might get a plum job in CID there.'

Peter Harridance followed Costello with his eyes as he went out to the street.

'Something eating him as usual?'

'Possibly. I got the impression he was hostile, but for no reason I could discover. Possibly racial – blacks and other outsiders getting all the plum jobs, you know the kind of thing. He didn't actually call me an uppitty nigger, but maybe he would have liked to.'

'Where does his surname come from, I wonder,' said Harridance with a wry smile. 'East Grinstead?'

Charlie raised his hand with a grin and went out to his car.

Once back at home Charlie pushed the button for Classic FM and sat down in his favourite chair and closed his eyes. He felt the need for music he knew by heart already, and for once he was not interested in reading the paper. It wasn't Ben Costello he wanted to think about: if the man had a problem with his, Charlie's, colour, that was something common enough in the police force not to need special attention. It was the boy at the nursery who hadn't gone to school that day who was jigging around on the outskirts of his brain. It was his mother who hadn't wanted him to go. But the medical reason, he felt quite sure, was Dwayne's invention. And if that was so there was surely a possibility that the reason was yesterday's death in the quarry. Why would an anxious mother tie that up with school? Or was it he, Charlie, who was doing the tying-up? Was he becoming incapable of seeing that not everything that happened in

Slepton Edge need have a connection with the event that was occupying most of his thoughts.

So Rupert Coggenhoe's death was now a 'case', like any other that he had been involved in. With one difference. It could not be investigated in the usual way, especially with Inspector Costello watching his every move.

He went to fetch Carola, convinced that the boy – or half of him – wanted to talk about his mother's worries but wouldn't necessarily take the initiative to talk even to a black policeman. He was going to have to take the first steps himself. Surely Costello couldn't object to his talking to a boy waiting to fetch his sister from nursery school, could he?

So while he was waiting for school to be over (and at least five minutes beyond that, because Carola always spent a lot of time on gossip with her friends before finally coming out to her parent waiting in the December air) he let his eyes go everywhere, as policemen so often have to. He was glad eventually to see the boy sauntering up to the gates of the little school. He waited till he was inside the garden, then went up to him and was interested to read a strange mixture of alarm and interest in his face.

'Hello. Still not gone back to school?'

The boy shrugged and mumbled 'Still not

feeling too good.'

Charlie's eyebrows shot up satirically.

'Really? I don't think your mum would let you fetch your sister if there was something really wrong.'

'Oh, it's nothing *really* wrong, nothing serious.'

'I think you want to be at school, don't you? School is a pretty good place to be for you drama geeks, isn't it?'

An ecstatic smile spread over the boy's face.

'Yeah. It's fun. And you never know: it might lead to something.'

'Of course it might. Would you rather be on the stage or on the box?'

'Oh, on the stage. More exciting. You get more of a buzz.'

'Now, the truth is, you want to go to school, don't you, but your mum doesn't want you to. That's rather unusual, isn't it?'

Dwayne shrugged again, but he was talking more confidently now.

'She gets funny ideas.'

'And this particular funny idea is about the drama stream, isn't it?'

'Well... Sort of... It's not police business though... I don't want to talk about it.'

'I think part of you does,' said Charlie, speaking low and gently. 'Part of you is worried too, isn't it?'

The boy shifted awkwardly from foot to foot.

'Maybe. But I'd never have thought of it if she hadn't come up with it. Daft old git.'

'She can't be that daft if what she's worried about is worrying you too. So what was it about?'

There was a long silence, then the boy took a deep breath.

'It's about the play, you see.'

'*The Tempest?*'

'No, not that one. We haven't done that one yet. She'd been to see it, you see. Not that you can really see a radio play. The acting's all in the voice.'

'Of course it is. Is that the one with the funny title?'

'That's right. *Unman, Wittering and Zigo.*'

'That's the one where the boys terrorise their teacher, isn't it?'

'Yes. Only with us it's boys and girls, to give them parts as well. It doesn't make much difference. It's a really good play.'

'I'm sure it is. So your mother came to see it?'

'That's right. Three months ago.'

'So why is she bringing it up now?'

That brought another long silence, then another deep breath.

'The children are terrorising this new teacher, you see. And one of the things they keep hinting at is what happened to their other teacher, the one this teacher is replacing.'

162

'I think I get you. So what did happen to him?'

Dwayne swallowed.

'They pushed him over a cliff.'

10

On the Scent

Charlie had ample time to meditate on the surprise information that Dwayne Vickery had handed him, and time too to wonder whether it was pure red herring or something that genuinely took him further. You could never rule out coincidence and in real life one sometimes encountered whopping ones. 'Quarry', 'cliff' – the differences weren't great, and certainly wouldn't be to the body going over the edge. But the likeness in the method of killing didn't necessarily point towards the children. Mrs Vickery had obviously been at a public performance of the play, so all sorts of other people could have been there too. Quite apart from the fact that, with apparently a great many children involved, the main outlines of the play's plot could have been known to half the village.

But that being so, why should anyone want to kill Rupert in such a way as to draw

163

attention to the drama stream at Westowram High? At least it was clear now why he had had that distraught visit from Harvey Buckworth that morning. Harvey had got the point immediately, even if he hadn't wanted to bring it out into the open to a policeman. Anyone actually involved with the drama classes would have wanted to direct attention *away* from it, not towards it.

No. Not necessarily. He was forgetting that they were, after all, children, the actors in that oddly-named play, and therefore would not think in the same way as adults, did not have the same self-protective shell which they could draw up to shield themselves in moments of danger. One of the children might have thought of it in some such terms as: it worked in the play so it might work in real life.

All this he chewed over with Felicity, when she got back from Leeds and teaching.

'I just can't work out whether it's a false trail, or something of real importance,' said Charlie, his face twisted with thought. 'And it may be connected to another thing that Costello brought up that I kick myself for not having thought of before.'

'What's that?'

'How did your father and Anne Michaels come together?'

'How does anyone?' said Felicity.

'Well, where: in the pubs, when she would

have been with her parents? In one of the shops? At school? Was Rupert asked to give a chat about his writing there? Did they get chatting on a walk? Has Anne Michaels got a dog, perhaps? Did she and her little gang target Rupert as an incomer? It seems an unlikely way of getting acquainted.'

Felicity nodded, and went off to bathe Carola, remaining thoughtful throughout the whole wet and noisy process. When she had got her to bed and to something approaching sleep she came back into the big room in the house and said to Charlie:

'I've had an idea about my dad and Anne Michaels.'

'Good, because I haven't. I can't even guess how they met.'

'Do you remember you came home during the evening one day, while you were busy with that copper's shooting? You went straight to bed, but you told me the next day that as you were coming in from the car you thought you heard the singing of the children's gang, and that it came roughly from the direction of Dad's bungalow?'

'That's right. Or rather the direction of Forsythia Avenue. Could have been anyone up there. Even Ben Costello lives somewhere near your dad, and they might have fingered him for an Italian immigrant.'

'I doubt it. People don't think about unusual names in Britain unless they're really unpronounceable, and Abbot and Costello have made it seem perfectly usual instead of Italian or Irish, or whatever it is. If he was fingered it was as a newcomer to the village. But say it was my dad, and they were up there singing their song "'Ban, 'Ban, Ca-Caliban", and maybe others too. What might my dad have thought?'

'That he was being serenaded as one of the country's foremost writers?'

'That they were carol singers.'

"'Ban, 'Ban, Ca-Caliban" doesn't sound much like a carol, especially the way they sing it.'

'My dad was tone deaf. I've often told you. He could barely distinguish the "National Anthem" from "Happy Birthday to You".'

Charlie pondered.

'So he goes to the door, the smaller children scatter, Anne stays there – pert little piece as she is – and she goes along with the carol singers idea, says the younger ones have gone home to bed, maybe gets invited in...'

'Yeah, well, the detail isn't important. But I do think that, or something very like it, could have been how it all started.'

And the more Charlie considered it, the more he liked it. And the more he thought, the more he saw how Anne Michaels could have acted up to the role that Rupert Coggenhoe would have cast her in: that of the acolyte, the admirer, the breathless fan.

Maybe at first she genuinely thought Rupert was a well-known writer who could be useful to her when she became a real actress. But perhaps always in the back of her mind there was the possibility of making real mischief for him, or using the threat of it as blackmail.

The next morning, Tuesday, Charlie was not on duty till eleven. Over coffee and toast he took up the Bradford telephone directory and looked up Vickery. There was only one in the Halifax area, and it was, he felt pretty sure, in the Slepton Edge district – a street five minutes from the centre. As Felicity was setting off for nursery school he got in the car, drove through the village, then left the car at the nearest wide road. He idled away a few minutes in a newsagent-cum-any-thing-with-a-better-profit-margin on the corner of Mitching Lane, where he felt sure the Vickerys would live. He was rewarded first by seeing Dwayne barge out of the front door and go off joyfully to school; then, a few minutes later, by seeing a sub-stantial black lady who reminded him of photographs of his mother when younger, leading a small girl. He paid for his *Times*, then drove his car to the nursery school, passing Felicity on her way home with a gaggle of young and youngish mothers.

He stopped his car when he saw Mrs Vickery on the way back from dropping off her daughter. Charlie got out and strolled up to her with a casual air.

'Do you think I could have a word with you?'

She looked at him, definitely flirtatious.

'If you care to walk with me to the bus stop round the corner, I'm on duty in half an hour.' She was a deep contralto, and spoke with a precise almost prissy accent.

'On duty?'

'At Halifax General Hospital.'

'Ah. This isn't professional. It was more in your capacity as a mother I wanted to talk.'

'Well, I have that capacity as well as that of Senior Nurse.' Suddenly the accent changed, though not the element of flirtation. 'If yo' ain't embarrassed to go talkin' to a black person who's gone up in de world, then I ain't de same. Even if yo' is a p'liceman.'

'Policeman and Senior Nurse,' said Charlie, smiling broadly back. 'Pretty similar jobs.'

'We in Nursing have to be much more tough.' The accent had become prissy again. 'Now, I don't know your name, but you sat in on the drama classes a while back, and gave them a talking-to afterwards. And you spoke to my boy Dwayne yesterday.'

'Right. And you kept him off school yesterday because you realised that questions might be asked about a death that resembled the one in *Unman, Whatsit and Whosit*.'

168

'I did.' She sighed. 'Oh, I knew I couldn't keep him home for long. For a start he'd sneak out, and I've a reputation for firmness to keep up. I just wanted to spare him getting involved in all the gossip and rumour that will be going round. He was one of the main boys in the play.'

'And do you think there's a connection?'

''Yo' is de copper, boy. But it's a hell of a coincidence, isn't it?'

'You're assuming it was murder, aren't you?'

This caused her to think long and hard.

'Well, yes, I am. If it wasn't a murder, or not a premeditated one, it doesn't seem so much of a coincidence.'

'Are you a bit suspicious of the drama stream for your boy? You wouldn't be the only one if you were.'

They came up to the bus stop and again she considered long before replying.

'I *wasn't* suspicious. Dwayne seemed so happy ... so *bright*. And he didn't fall behind in the other subjects either – got better at them, in fact. But I heard from some of the other mothers that kids from the other streams were jealous, that there was a lot of bad blood, a feeling that the drama stream was getting way above themselves. I didn't want that for Dwayne. And then there was this nasty little gang. They could have picked on me next, and *wouldn't* I have given them hell, and Dwayne too.'

'I think they'd have thought twice before they picked on you,' said Charlie.

'Maybe. But children aren't as wise and cautious as adults. And then came this death. Maybe I'm being silly, but it made me think. And I'm not daft enough to think that all the children in the stream are going to end up with a career on stage or on telly, or directing or designing or whatever. Most of them will end up loading shelves in Marks and Spencer's, just like the other kids. It doesn't do to burn your bridges with most of the other pupils in the school.'

Charlie nodded. She was a feet-on-the-ground lady.

'This little gang – it's been active round our way.'

'Has it? Didn't pick on you, then, with your Brixton accent. You'd give them a hefty wallop if they did, I bet you.'

'Policemen are the last people who can go around giving kids a hefty wallop. Now, the gang is led by Anne Michaels I know.'

'Oh, there's no doubt about that. Stuck up little miss. And dangerous I'd guess.'

'You're not far out there. I'll maybe talk to her later. I'd like to talk to one of the younger children first. Know any of them?'

'One or two. I guess they'll be frightened of talking. Not of you so much as of her. She'll have put the fear of God into them, if

170

I know her.'

'Who would you recommend I talk to?'

She ran through the children in her head.

'I've seen them hanging around together, so I know most of them by sight. One I do know better than that is Carmel Postgate. She was in hospital for a couple of weeks with pneumonia earlier this year. The pneumonia didn't stop her chattering away nineteen to the dozen every minute the day held.' She looked at Charlie. 'That could be useful, I guess. Right. This is my bus.'

'One more thing,' said Charlie quickly. 'Could you forget we've had this conversation? Pretend it's never happened?'

'Sure. It'll be a secret between you and me and the twenty or thirty people who've passed us in the street.'

And she waved cheerily as she got on the bus.

Charlie walked thoughtfully back to the car. Of course he had been careless. But where could he have gone to talk to Mrs Vickery in secret? He didn't particularly care if Costello found out he'd been talking to possible witnesses *eventually*. He could cope with that, if the information he had gathered proved relevant. He had no particular sympathy with policemen who cared about their patch and their promotion over the calls of the case and securing a just result. But he didn't want it to come out now, with all the

171

possible repercussions including disciplinary ones. He was going to have to be more discreet.

He drove carefully through Westowram, where parents and toddlers were still making their way to school, then out towards the M62 to Leeds and work. But he was not two minutes from the centre when he thought he saw Chris Carlson. This was not surprising when he was making his way to somewhere local to paint. But today he was going nowhere. He was removing rubbish from an old corner shop that looked as if it had been closed for decades and was well on the path to dereliction. As he slowed and watched, Chris and a teenage boy brought out ancient tills, bits of a counter, even groceries presumably spectacularly past their sell-by date. He was rather ashamed as he watched Chris, in his shirt-sleeves on a coldish winter morning, because his mind was estimating whether he was physically capable of tipping Rupert Coggenhoe over the quarry edge. There was no question about it: he was six foot, lean, very lithe. There would be no contest if he was faced with a seventy-year-old man, gone to seed, with a stoop and a prominent tummy.

Charlie got out of his car and went over.

'Setting up shop?' he asked pleasantly.

'Charlie!' said Chris, stopping work and mopping his brow. 'Wasn't expecting you.

Not exactly shop, more like office. It was a shop once, but it's been closed for years. I've rented it for a couple of months, with an option. It's going to be my campaign head-quarters. Alison wasn't keen on the office being at home – not with her being about to produce the long-awaited offspring in four months' time.'

'I can understand that. So you've decided?'

'Yes, I have. I felt as if it decided itself, was inevitable, after my having got so close last time. I felt as if I'd be breaking faith with all those who'd supported me then. And the truth is, I enjoyed the campaigning that time, and I'm looking forward to it now. It's something worth doing.'

'I think I'd keep quiet about it for a bit,' said Charlie.

'Keep quiet? How can you keep an election campaign quiet?'

'I mean for a week or two. He's only been dead three or four days. People might see it as you jumping rather over-enthusiastically into a dead man's shoes.'

Christ looked gobsmacked for a moment.

'Good Lord, I hadn't thought of that. Tasteless, you feel?'

'A bit. And pushy.'

'I wouldn't want to be that. It wouldn't do me any good at all... Peter!' He called in the direction of the boy, who was struggling with a long plank of wood. 'I think you'd better do the removal work. I'll stay inside and give the place a lick of paint.'

'It'll cost you,' said Peter stoutly. 'If I'm going to do all that lifting work I'll need an increase of wages.'

'Oh, all right,' said Chris reluctantly. 'I promised you eight pounds for the morning. We'll say ten.'

'Twelve.'

'Why you– Oh all right. It's daylight robbery, though. I'm only giving it you because you've got me over a barrel.'

Chris made himself less public by slipping inside. Charlie and Peter followed him, and watched as he took up a paint pot and brush.

'Know a girl named Carmel Postgate?' he asked Chris. 'Quite young – eleven, twelve maybe.'

'I don't,' said Chris, stirring the paint. 'Children don't come to me with their worries.'

'Maybe they should.'

'I know her,' said Peter, glad of any excuse to put off heavy work. 'Chatters like a parrot – you can't shut her up.'

'I heard that. She goes to Westowram High I suppose. First or second year.'

'That's right. Drama stream. They make you sick, that lot. Go on as if they're God's gift to the nation. She's one of Anne Michaels's little followers. What a crew! You watch she doesn't take you on next. Incomers is what they go for, and it's often as not colour they're really talking about.'

'Know where Carmel Postgate lives?'

'Up Brigg Street. It'll be about number eighteen or twenty. Father works in the Council Offices.'

'Right. Thank you very much. I'd like you to keep quiet about this. I don't want it to get around for a bit.'

'It'll cost you.'

Charlie sighed, pulled out his wallet, and handed over a fiver.

It was some way into the afternoon, when he was deep in the paperwork connected to the shooting of the police sergeant and the charge against his assailant, that Charlie got an idea. Politicians were then, as always, proclaiming how they would reduce paperwork for the police while they were at the same time bringing in new regulations that would increase it further. The only thing that Charlie would say in favour of the mountain of forms he was compelled to produce was that most of them could be filled in with only half a mind.

When the idea occurred to him he grabbed the phone.

'Felicity? I want you to do something.'

'Something to do with Dad's death?'

'Yes. How did you know?'

'Tone of voice. You wouldn't use that tone or those words if you just wanted me to go down to the supermarket for a bottle of Teachers. Anyway you always get that tone when you're on a murder case.'

'Don't use that word. Nobody's sure, not even me.'

'But the others think the balance of probability is to natural causes, and you think the balance is towards unnatural causes.'

'Maybe. Shut up. I'm supposed to be working. There's a girl called Carmel Postgate, lives up Brigg Street, maybe number eighteen or twenty. They'll probably be in the directory.'

'You say "girl". I presume you mean one of the younger children in Anne Michaels's gang?'

'Yes. Very bubbly and talkative.'

'Sounds useful.'

'But don't bank on it. A lot of talk about the murder has probably gone around the school, so she might be a bit reserved. There's the parents too. Many of them must have seen *Unman, Whosit and Whatsit*, and if connections are being made at school they very likely will be made at home too. So Carmel's parents may be protective too.'

'All right, all right. You don't have to mollycoddle me. I take it you want me to go round and talk to her and find out if the gang ever targeted my dad, and if so what happened when they went up to sing songs at him.'

'Exactly.'

'Anything else?'

'Just anything your novelist's antennae can pick up about the dynamics of the gang, or about its leader.'

'It shall be done. I'll enjoy doing it.'

Gaining admittance to the Postgate home was easier than Felicity expected. Even before her father's death their arrival in the village had been generally noticed – Charlie's colour, the fact that he was an inspector, Felicity's own ambitions to be a novelist 'like her father' (the phrase, commonly used, would have driven Felicity wild if she had heard it) meant that they were a marked family. She was therefore invited in, Carola was sent to play in a back room with Carmel's pre-school-age brother, and they could settle down in the sitting room.

'It's my father,' said Felicity. 'I'm still trying to come to terms with his death, you see.'

'It must be awful when it's so sudden.'

'It is. Much more difficult to make sense of. You must be wondering what it has to do with you.'

'Well ... not altogether. But go on.'

'It's really your daughter Carmel I wanted to talk to.'

An expression of aggravation crossed Mrs Postgate's face.

'I thought as much! She'll be home any time now.' She leaned forward confidingly. 'She's clammed up every time your dad's death has been mentioned, and Jim and I have been convinced there's been something up – something connected with that Anne Michaels we feel sure. She's such a bossy little madam, and we're sure she's been leading the younger ones astray. What's a girl of her age doing, spending so much time with kids three or four years younger than herself?'

There was a sound of a key in the front door, and someone entering. There had for some time been a degree of noise and childish laughter from the kitchen, suggesting that Carola and the young Postgate were getting on fine. Soon there came a child's voice raised: 'Mummy, who's this black kid Dicky's playing with?'

A face peered round the door, and its jaw dropped.

'Don't be so rude, Carmel,' said Mrs Postgate, red with embarrassment. 'This is Mrs Peace, whose father died – you know, Mr Coggenhoe. She'd like to have a talk with you.'

The supposedly talkative girl clammed up at once, an obstinate expression settling on her face. 'I don't want to talk to her.'

'Oh yes you will, my girl,' said her mother, no mean exponent of the obstinate expression herself. 'You'll tell her exactly what she wants to know.'

The girl came in, dragging her feet, and went to sit on the sofa under the window, as far as possible from Felicity.

'I don't know anything,' she muttered.

'You don't know anything about what?' Felicity asked sweetly.

'Nothing.'

It looked like being a long haul unless Felicity came straight to the point, so that's what she did.

'I suppose you mean you don't know anything about this little ... group that Anne Michaels has got together from children in the drama stream, don't you?'

After a long pause Carmel nodded.

'Now, I'm not going to get you into trouble, or to blame you in any way. I just want to know about the last weeks of my father's life. Do you understand?' Another nod. 'Now, this little group has been going round to newcomers in the village, singing outside their houses, shouting through their letter-boxes and so on, haven't they? Haven't you?'

'We didn't mean no harm. It was just fun.'

'Not much fun for the Nortons I'm told, nor for anyone else you've targeted. But like I say, I'm not here to blame. Newcomers are a bit of a soft target I suppose. You never got on to us, though.'

'Your husband's a policeman. Otherwise Anne says we would've.'

179

'I can imagine. But instead of us you picked on my dad.'

Again a pause, and then a nod.

'Now, you went up there one evening, a week or two ago, didn't you?'

By now the obstinate expression had softened.

'Yes... We all knew who he was. People pointed him out.'

'They did, I know. Then you all gathered outside his bungalow, didn't you, in the dark?'

Carmel suddenly became almost voluble, caught up in the excitement.

'That was the part we liked. It was wonderful. Like we were just dark shapes if he looked out the window, just inside his gate.'

'And you sang the song from *The Tempest*, didn't you?'

'Yes. That's just right – really nasty-sounding, though nobody really knows what it means. It's ever such an old play. Then we sang the song that Anne made up to the tune of "Onward, Christian Soldiers". It starts: "Go back where you came from".'

'Charming. What happened next?'

'There was a light came on in the hall, and there was this shape coming towards the door.'

'What did you do?'

'Ran out the gate and scattered. That's what Anne had told us to do, and what we'd always done. Then even if they realise it was children outside they can't iden– i-den-ti-fy which children. So we waited, all separate, down or up the street. The door opened. But it was different to the usual, and we heard voices, and then we realised that Anne hadn't run away.'

'No. She stayed there and talked to my father, didn't she?'

'Yes. And then the door shut, and Anne still didn't come out. So we all went home, because it was nearly nine o'clock. But we were worried in case he'd done something horrible to her. He hadn't though. She turned up at school the next day, so it was all right.'

'What did she say happened?'

Carmel by now was well into her narrative stride.

'Wouldn't say. Said the silly old git– Sorry – the old man thought we were carol singers. Pretty funny carol, "'Ban, 'Ban, Ca-Caliban".'

'My father was tone deaf,' said Felicity.

'What does that mean?'

'That you can't tell one tune from another. Just like some people are word-blind – they can't manage words, and others can't manage numbers. Music just meant nothing to my dad.'

'I can't do arithmetic, or hardly,' said Carmel.

'There you are, you see. So my dad got it

wrong and thought you were only on a friendly visit to sing carols. So did you ever hear what happened after Anne went inside?'

'No. She just said we wouldn't be going there again.'

'What did you think happened?'

'Some of us thought they went to bed together, but I didn't, not with an old man like he was. I think they just liked each other, because they were talking together at the carol service.'

'That's quite likely.'

'Anyway, I expect Anne got something out of it.'

'Something out of it? What sort of thing?'

But though she wheeled and threatened, Felicity never got a straight answer as to what Anne got out of her encounters. After a time she just said 'I must take my black child home' and left.

11

A Bought Peace

That evening Charlie came off duty at eight, and drove home for a late steak and chips, followed by an account from Felicity of her conversation with Carmel Postgate and her

182

mother. He was slumped out on the sofa and looking forward to coffee (wondering, at the same time, whether it was too early to go to bed), when the doorbell rang.

'Must be Chris,' he shouted to Felicity in the kitchen. 'Who else would call so late?'

But when he went to open the front door he found it was a couple whom he had no memory of.

'Mr Peace?' began the man. 'You don't know me but you–'

'Mr – ah! – Norton. Mr Norton from the Hatton Homes estate.'

'You recognised the voice. I can tell you're a policeman. Mr Peace, I don't want to intrude, because I know you and your wife have suffered a bereavement–'

'No, no. Come in,' said Charlie, standing aside. 'I'd be interested to hear how things have gone since we talked. Here is my wife. Felicity, this is the Nortons.'

He ushered them in, sat them down on the sofa, and Felicity went to the kitchen to fetch coffee, taking care to leave both doors open. They were an appealing-looking pair – pleasant rather than distinguished in any way. In their early sixties, Charlie guessed, and now much more confident and relaxed than when he had spoken to Mr Norton on the phone. He and his wife were both looking around them, interested in the house, and hardly at all tensed up.

'I'd make a guess and say you've come through the business with the children and it's now all quiet on the Norton front – am I right?' said Charlie.

The Nortons both grinned.

'Well, that's about right. I'm Richard, by the way, and the wife's Carol. Yes, we have come through.'

'Good. I'd be interested to hear how.'

'That's partly why we're here – to tell you. The truth is, you see, that we're getting about in Slepton Edge a lot more now, talking to people in shops, going to the pub now and then, and what people are talking about at the moment is the death of your – father-in-law, was it?'

'That's right. Felicity's father.'

'We were very sorry to hear about it, because we're so grateful for what you did for us.'

'I did nothing that did any good,' said Charlie. 'The story of quite a lot of a policeman's life. But I did try.'

'The truth is that people are gossiping rather than just talking. You know how gossip always magnifies everything, and links up all sorts of things that aren't connected. Well, people were talking in the pub at lunchtime, and they were linking up the death of Mr Coggenhoe – my wife has read some of his books, enjoyed them very much – linking his death up with the drama stream at Westowram High. Is that right?'

'I believe so,' said Charlie cautiously. 'Not that there's anything in it, necessarily. They're talking because a radio play that the drama kids did in class and then in public had in it a man pushed over a cliff.'

'Doesn't seem much of a connection.'

'Pushed over by the boys in his class.'

'Even so... But I'm not a literary type, and not a detective either.'

'If you had asked us a couple of weeks ago,' put in Carol Norton, 'we'd probably have said that we wouldn't put anything past that nasty little gang. Things are a bit different now.'

'So I gather,' said Charlie. 'Tell me what happened.'

Felicity had come in with the coffee, and started to hand it round. Richard Norton waited till everyone had a cup, then took up his story.

'Well, it was about five days after I spoke to you on the telephone. There was a ring on the doorbell about four o'clock in the afternoon. It wasn't yet dark, but it was getting that way, so I opened the door a bit cautiously. And there was this girl – young woman it almost seemed – standing there bold as brass.'

'You recognised her?'

'Not to say recognised. You see they'd always come at night, and I'd only seen them by peering through our bedroom window. Sometimes a street light caught one of their faces, but not often. But I thought it was one of the two elder girls – I think her name is Anne Michaels.'

'And we weren't in doubt for long,' put in his wife.

'No, we weren't. Because she simply said, without so much as a "hello" or telling me her name: "Can I come in? I've got a proposition to make to you".'

Charlie's eyebrows hit the roof.

'I wasn't expecting that.'

The couple nodded.

'Nor were we, I can tell you,' said Richard Norton. 'Anyway, I wasn't happy about her coming into the house, and I hesitated, but she just pushed past me and marched into the lounge. I protested, but ... well, I've never been a very forceful chap, and she took no notice.'

'I was already in the lounge,' said Carol Norton, 'listening. She came straight in, didn't even nod to me, and sat down in one of our easy chairs. And when Richard got back into the room she looked at him and said: 'I suppose you'd like an end to these visits from the children, wouldn't you?' And before Richard could reply I said 'We would'. I didn't want any macho stuff from him, posturing like, because the truth was I wanted to do anything she asked us to do, just to get rid of them.'

'As if I could manage a macho posture if I tried!' protested Richard. 'Anyway, she grinned an evil grin – such a shame, because she is naturally such a lovely looking girl – and said: "It can't be nice having a pack of kids shouting and singing at you. I expect you've always liked children, haven't you?" And I said "I used to". She liked that, and grinned still more.'

'I'm still puzzled,' said Felicity. 'I still don't have any idea of what she was after.'

'Oh, it didn't take long for that to come out,' said Carol. 'She took up Richard's last remark straight away – she seems to be a very quick-witted girl. She said: "You could start liking them again, I should think, if you got rid of us".'

'I said "maybe",' said Richard. 'Because at that moment it seemed like she'd changed my view of children for life.'

'She took that up too, didn't she, Richard? She said "We're not the usual run of snotty-nosed kids, you know. We're out of the ordinary". And Richard said "You're certainly that". I sat there hoping that was the last of his smart-alec remarks, because I was afraid she would take offence and leave.'

'Well, she didn't,' said Richard. 'She'd come with a purpose, that was obvious, and she was determined to get it before she left. I said: "What will it take for you to leave us alone?" And she said "What will it *cost* is really the question". I thought: "I can't believe this is just a common-or-garden piece of blackmail". But that's what it was.'

'It would be interesting to know if you're the first to be stung like that,' said Charlie, thoughtfully. 'Has she had a whole line of victims? Sorry – go on.'

'Well, she was sitting there, smiling like a Cheshire tiger, and I just said: "How much?" And she paused, licked her tongue around her lips, and said "Twenty pounds". You could have knocked me down with a feather. I was expecting five times as much.'

'I said "Done!"' said Carol. 'I got up, went to Richard's wallet, got out a note and handed it to her.'

'Did she look disappointed?' asked Charlie. 'As if she wished she'd asked for more?'

'No,' said Richard. 'If she was, she didn't let it show. She gave a little smile of satisfaction, put it in the pocket of her school blazer, and got up. "Nice to have done business with you," she said, and as she went through the door: "We won't be back".'

'Well,' said Charlie, stretching back in his chair and taking a deep breath, 'I'm as flabbergasted as you are. As a policeman I can't approve of giving way to blackmail. Still, I'd have to admit that you got off lightly. It seems so out of character. Do we put it down to a child's ignorance of money – twenty pounds seeming an awful lot to her?'

'Mr Peace, we have grandchildren,' said Carol Norton. 'These days kids have a very good idea of what money is worth and what it will buy. And I'm sure this particular young woman has a much better idea than most.'

'Come along Carol, it's getting late,' said her husband, standing up. 'We've done what we came to do. I just hope it's useful, if there is a connection between the children and your dad's death, Mrs Peace.'

'I do think there's a connection,' said Felicity.

'I wish there was a way we could say "thank you",' said Mrs Norton. 'It was so good to have someone who was on our side.'

'Didn't you say you were a baker?' Charlie said to Mr Norton. He nodded. 'It would be good to have a nice loaf of bread, baked by someone who really knows what he's doing. We've tried more than once, but the results are always dismal.'

'Even when Charlie is kneading,' said Felicity, 'and bashes the living daylights out of the dough.'

'Oh, you have to do it with love,' said Norton. 'Aggression is no good with bread at all. You'll have one of my best farm-houses, and a brown one too, and it'll be our pleasure.'

When they had gone Charlie and Felicity

chewed over the cud provided by the Nortons.

'I'm sure Norton is right about Anne Michaels. She is the sort of young lady who is bound to be on the ball where money is concerned. So why did she call off the persecution and settle for so little?'

'You'd been to the school and read the riot act,' said Felicity. 'She could have seen her glittering career stymied from the start by a police investigation.'

'I wish I'd been so effective,' said Charlie. 'I didn't get that impression at the time. There is a rather mundane explanation that occurs to me. I guess that the drama pupils are a lot busier than most of the children at Westowram High: rehearsals and special classes after school, in addition to all the usual school work and homework. Time to – let's say – amuse themselves – must be limited. Maybe they wanted to be off with those not-particularly-interesting (to them) people as quickly as they could because they'd got a more interesting and potentially profitable victim in view.'

'My dad?'

'Yes. This was probably about the time they targeted him and I heard them singing when I came home from work.'

Felicity thought.

'Or a slightly different interpretation,' she said: 'they'd already been there by the time

Anne called on the Nortons. Anne had been invited in, and had had the idea for a new sort of blackmail, something much more subtle, which didn't involve a posse of young children.'

'Rather demeaning in the long term for a fifteen/sixteen-year-old, you think, to run around with a children's gang, even if she was the leader?'

'Exactly. She gets a sum she can share among her little army, tells them she's too busy with *The Tempest* to do anything for a bit, and then embarks on establishing a relationship with Dad. After a time she starts making the connection with him a bit more public.'

'At the carol service, for example.'

'At the carol service. Where, alas, she was helped by me. Not to mention that poor old Dad fell for it like a sucker.'

'I never thought of your dad as a sucker. More of a predator.'

'Yes, with Mum he was, capitalising on her devotion. And anyone else who enjoyed being a doormat. But he never knew how the mass of ordinary people thought or reacted. That made him very vulnerable.'

'What you're saying is that Anne intended to capitalise one way or another on the suspicion and shock ordinary people would feel at a close relationship between an elderly novelist and a fifteen-year-old schoolgirl.'

'I can't think of a better motive for her getting involved with him. She was aiming to create the sort of shock that swept through Coombe Barton. Anne's parents hadn't felt it by the time that Dad died, but their slowness could have been prodded by Anne herself, with well-calculated "revelations".'

They left it there. Charlie found it hard to envisage Rupert Coggenhoe as a victim, but it did seem plausible that Anne Michaels should have intended making him one.

The next morning, before he went to work, he had a phone call from Ben Costello. It was not very satisfactory.

'Inspector Peace? I'm ringing about the autopsy on your father-in-law.'

Charlie made no comment on the 'Inspector Peace', but instead kept his cool, conspicuously.

'Do you want to speak to Felicity?'

'No, I think it will be better to talk to you first. As far as the initial findings are concerned, they're inconclusive. As I think we said was likely to be the case, there were so many injuries to the body as it fell from the upper path to the bottom of the quarry that distinguishing any particular blow by human hand was extremely difficult. But, of course, work is continuing on that.'

'I see. Rather as I expected.'

'As I did too. Now my boss, Superintendent Trench, is keen to get possible DNA material from the clothing and send it for analysis. Mr Coggenhoe was wearing an old sports jacket that would respond. But I must say I don't see the point of all that if we have no suspicion of foul play.'

'What exactly do you mean?'

'Well, say we get material that connects this Anne Michaels to him, or for that matter connects your wife to him, would it tell us anything we don't already know? They were both close to him, and could well have handled his clothing. But I'm not the one in charge. All I'm doing is telling you a possible step that we may take in the future. And as you know it could involve a long wait.'

'Don't I know it,' said Charlie feelingly.

'You might like to make your feelings known to Superintendent Trench, who's in charge of the case.'

'No, I wouldn't. My motto in such cases is to tread softly. It's his business entirely, so far as I'm concerned. I'll get Felicity. This is her loss and her problem, so her views are the ones you want.'

'Oh – before you get her, I believe you've been talking to the Vickerys – Dwayne and his mother.'

'I was just going to tell you that,' lied Charlie. 'I know the boy from the visit I made to the drama class at the High School here. You must have heard the rumour that's going around the village: that my father-in-law's death is connected – I suppose you could almost say inspired – by the death of one of the characters in a play put on by the drama stream.'

'I had heard,' said Costello, with contempt in his voice. 'I think more than enough has been said about those kids. As I probably made clear when we talked.' Charlie's face was impassive, and he continued regardless.

'I was alerted to the possibility of gossip by an odd visit I had from Harvey Buckworth, who is one of the stream's teachers. I managed to get out of Dwayne what was worrying Buckworth, which he never came clean about himself. I told Mrs Vickery it all seemed very far-fetched, and she really shouldn't be keeping her son off school as a result of loose talk such as this.'

'I'm not worried about her bloody son. All this talk will do is send people off on the wrong track. By now ninety per cent of the village will be convinced it was a murder, whereas accident or suicide are much more likely explanations.'

'I'd agree with you about accident – heart attack, leading to a fall. No indication of that though in the post-mortem?'

'None so far.'

'But I can't agree about suicide. No one who knew my father-in-law will believe he could consider robbing the world of his incomparable gifts by taking his own life.'

'Maybe. You could be a bit biased, don't you think? There could be reasons we know nothing about. Anyway, I'm relying on you keeping out of this, like we said. It's probably not a case in any sensational sense of the word, but the last thing we need is Leeds sticking its nose into our business. Now, can I talk to your wife?'

Charlie put down the phone without saying another word, and called Felicity. He listened in to her end of the conversation, and his wife reacted exactly as he had done. He hoped that Ben Costello was more tactful and less aggressive in his part of the dialogue than he had been with him.

While they were still talking he went out and got into his car. On an impulse he drove towards Leeds by way of the road where Chris Carlson had set up his campaign headquarters. It had had a coat of paint around the windows and on the shopboard above the windows and doors. So far it was blank, but in the window there was a smart homemade poster simply shouting 'CARLSON FOR MAYOR'. As he drove past he saw the boy whom Chris had called Peter wielding an enthusiastic paintbrush inside the shop. He stopped his car and went back. The door was open and he stood a moment looking.

'Hi Peter. You having fun?'

The boy turned round and grinned.

'Yeah. I really like painting. I'm thinking of doing it for a living.'

Chris solving people's life problems for them again!

'Is Chris around?'

'Not now. He will be. He's gone to Radio Bradford to tell them about the mayor thing.'

'The mayor thing?'

'Like how it ought to be elected, how it hasn't yet been tried properly, and how the other system just produces party hacks.'

So much for playing it softly and slowly until Archie Skelton had been lowered into his grave. Chris went his own path, that was for sure.

'He's taught you all the words, hasn't he?' said Charlie mildly.

'He tried what he was going to say out on me yesterday. He made it sound good. I don't really know what a hack is, though.'

'It's somebody who just does all the dreary work and doesn't have an original idea in him.'

'Oh... Does Chris have original ideas?'

'Yes, I'd say he does.'

'He's not doing what you said about lying low. When people come in here – curious like – he gives them all this stuff about new ideas and party hacks.'

'Well, he doesn't have to take my advice. What's the reaction?'

'It varies. Some are enthusiastic, some less so. Somebody told him he shouldn't speak ill of the dead... When he comes back he's going to paint "CARLSON FOR MAYOR" on the shopboard over the door. I've got a lot of posters here for if anyone comes in and seems like a supporter.'

'Well, well. Chris could be right or wrong. He's so bloody charming he'll probably win over the doubters. I hope he's paying you.'

'Yeah. He's paying me ten pounds a morning for painting. I like it. It's better than school.'

Charlie didn't doubt it. He did wonder whether Chris was wise to employ a boy obviously bunking school and pay him well under the minimum wage.

When he got into work he rang Felicity before getting down to a new case involving teenagers shoplifting on a council estate.

'Did you listen to Radio Bradford this morning?' he asked her.

'No, I listened to the *Today* programme till I got fed up with that bossy woman, then I switched to Radio Three.'

'Never mind. Chris was on, though – talking about keeping the Mayor's job elective. I wondered how it had gone.'

'How do you know he was on?'

'I talked to the boy at his campaign headquarters. So far as I can see Chris is going all out from the word Go.'

'Isn't that what you advised him against?'

'Yes. But who takes advice from a policeman? I wouldn't. I'll hold my tongue in future. How did the conversation go with Ben Costello?'

'I think I told him pretty much what you told him.'

'You did. I listened to the first part.'

'Be my guest. So what do you want to know?'

'Was he aggressive, like he was with me?'

'Not aggressive. Sort of contemptuous. There was a sneer in his voice, like he despises all women. Probably sleeps around so he can share his contempt more widely. I do hope you get this case right, Charlie, and he gets it wrong.'

'I'll do my best to oblige. Getting him to acknowledge there is, or could well be, a *case* here would be a start.'

He could hear Felicity thinking.

'I can see the problem of proving a murderous attack. And what else could justify spending much time or money on it? And getting into DNA testing will probably take a lot of both and still not give the police anything conclusive.'

'Maybe.'

'Seems to me if Ben Costello has his way there will be no case to investigate, and if it gets to DNA testing there will still be no case to investigate... Charlie. Going back to Chris.

There's something that's been jiggling round in the back of my mind for a while now, and I've finally brought it to the front, and worked out why it's been bothering me.'

'Oh? What is it?'

'It's something I forgot to tell you in all the ... fuss. I had a visit from Alison the morning after the carol service. The day Dad died as it turned out. And the topic of Chris's "mission" came up – if that's what you call it. We talked about how people found it helpful to talk over their problems with him, and Alison said: "Chris loves it all. It's part of the healing process". And I think even at the time something clicked in my brain.'

'Ye-e-es.'

'And I've just realised what clicked, because it was as if she was saying it was part of the healing process for *Chris*.'

Charlie thought that over.

'Certainly when you said it now it sounded a bit odd. But that's totally out of context of course.'

'But Charlie, when you think about it Chris usually talks over people's problems and dilemmas, but there's no obvious *healing process* for the people who come to him as a rule.'

'Hmmm. Maybe not as a rule. But say there was someone who'd had a big tragedy in their life – say a bereavement – I could imagine them coming to Chris, and him helping them to come to terms with it.'

'Maybe... Charlie, how much do we know about Chris?'

'I should think I know exactly what you know.'

'It's not much, then, is it? I'd *like* to know: where does he come from? Where did he practise as a GP? Where was he a hospital consultant? Did he really give up his job because he was fed up with conditions in the National Health Service?'

'That's what he told us. In general we know what he's told us, and we don't know what he hasn't told us.'

'But wouldn't you think that by now we'd know where he grew up? Know where he practised medicine? I do.'

'So do I, though you've got to remember he has a very neutral, middle-of-the-road accent. It gives nothing away. I shout London, he shouts nothing.'

'He says nothing too. I know it has nothing to do with my dad's death, but I think we should learn more about Chris Carlson.'

12

The Man From Nowhere

An opportunity to learn more of Chris's background came a couple of days later, when he knocked on the door of Charlie and Felicity's house in Walsh Street and came in, flourishing a bit of paper in Felicity's face.

'I say, I'm sorry to trouble you, but could you take a look at this? There's a lot of pernickety old retired people around here who worry about "who" when it should be "whom".'

'I don't know anyone who worries about that any longer. Languages change, and "whom" is approaching its sell-by date. But there are people who feel very strongly about "may" and "might", not to mention "lay" and "lie". So what is this, then?'

'It's a sort of election address. An appeal to the voters. This is the bit where I tell them about myself.'

Felicity had expected something of the sort, and they took the statement over to the sofa where Charlie was sitting reading *The Times*, and together they went through it. This was the sort of opportunity that

Charlie was longing for.

CHRIS CARLSON –
THIS IS WHO I AM

I have lived in Slepton Edge now for three years, and thanks to the warm welcome I've received from the people I feel already that I belong here. Now I want to offer myself for the second time in the election for mayor of Halifax, because I am anxious for this chance to serve the citizens of the town as a whole.

I resigned from my hospital job because I saw which way the National Health Service was going: the family doctor was a dying breed; at hospitals even those with serious illnesses were treated on a conveyor-belt system. Worse is threatened now. Monster medical centres will replace the old surgeries and health centres. They will have people who can treat every imaginable illness, but there will be nobody there who can look at the whole person behind his medical problems. The same is true in so many areas: in education schools have got bigger, and each pupil becomes a tiny speck on a screen. In crime the policemen toil away producing statistics. They're never seen on the streets.

We need a new way, where the individual comes first.
VOTE FOR ME ON FEB –!

'A lot of people won't like "policemen" for "policemen and women", you know,' said Felicity. 'And *"his* medical problems".'

'I thought that was grammatically OK,' said Chris.

'We're not talking grammar, we're talking people's sensibilities.'

'Is this the statement you put out last time?' asked Charlie.

'Well, along the same lines. Don't you like it?'

'I suppose since it worked last time it must be OK. But I'd have said this isn't a CV at all – not a comprehensive bio. It doesn't tell the voters anything about you or what you've done. It's more a policy statement, or a rallying cry.'

'But surely they will all want to know where I stand?'

'First of all they'll want to know about you. How old are you? Where do you come from? How long did you practise medicine? How do you make your living now?'

Chris screwed up his face.

'A lot of those things would act against me, I should think. If I proclaim the fact that I'm a southerner, even a reformed one, they'll think of me as a carpet-bagger. Then again, what will they think if I say I earn my living by selling pictures? I'd guess they'll class me as the next thing to a door-to-door salesman or a gypsy. I think there's a lot to be said for vagueness.'

Charlie shook his head, with the certainty of one who has been much longer in the north.

'But as the campaign hots up you'll be forced to tell them more. The big parties will make sure of that. If it's not them, it'll be the punters. You'll be glad-handing it in the street, or raising your pint mug in the pub, and someone will ask you where you came from, what your father did for a living, how you met Alison.'

'Why should it matter to them whether I come from X or Y?'

'It fills in the picture.'

'What if I told them to mind their own business?'

'They'll say it is their business. You made it so by standing for election. And you'll have lost one and probably more votes.'

Chris stood, his fingers rubbing his chin, considering.

'Well, I'll think it over.'

'Do,' said Charlie, keeping the conversation light. 'There's a thin line between *not* telling people about something, and concealing it. I'm sure you've no intention of concealing, but if you ask me it would be dangerous to *seem* to be doing so.'

'Good point. Well, thanks for your help. See you soon.'

And he went off bearing the biography

that wasn't really a biography at all. Neither Charlie nor Felicity was surprised a few days later to see copies of it on the counter of the village supermarket with a 'police-women' and a 'her' inserted, but otherwise unchanged.

'Well, he did only come to consult you on the wording,' said Charlie.

'True. But it's odd, isn't it, that he claims to be the people's candidate, but he's not listening to anyone.'

It was next day, from Police Headquarters in Leeds, that Charlie rang his old boss, ex-Superintendent Oddie, now retired and running a model-train shop in a shopping mall near Hebden Bridge. The voice rang out louder and livelier than when he was burdened by his regular job.

'Charlie! Wonderful to hear from you! I was going to ring you when I read in the local paper of your bereavement, but then I thought that you and Felicity were hardly likely to be bowed down with grief, so I didn't know what tone of voice to adopt.'

'Ever the sensitive cop,' said Charlie, grinning with pleasure at re-establishing contact. 'No, we're not bowed down, but the fact that the cause of death is not yet established is troubling us.'

'Really? I thought he'd just stumbled over, after perhaps a glass or two too much at Sunday lunch.'

'You could still be right. I'm willing to bet that wasn't the case, though that's sheer guesswork-cum-experience, and I'm not letting on to the local Halifax cop, who doesn't seem interested in the murder possibility. Mike, does your retirement give you any spare time? Are you interested in using your police contacts to find out a few things for us?'

'Sure, I'd enjoy it. But what's stopping you? Oh, of course. It's the Rupert Coggenhoe business and you're too close, right?'

'Right. No question of my being involved in any way at all. And with the Halifax man being in a "you keep off my territory" mood, I'm having to be very careful. I'd rather not speak on the phone. Would it be all right if I came over?'

'Look forward to it. Do we make a date and time?'

'Difficult, work being what it is. But there's no great urgency. I'll drop by in the next few days.'

But as it turned out it was the next day when Charlie found himself in Luddenden, and when his job was done he drove in the direction of Hebden Bridge and the disused mill just outside it which had smartened itself up into a collection of boutiques and specialist shops. He parked his car, then lingered over the shops nearest the entrance, all aiming to be Harvey Nicks if only they had the money and the flair. Five minutes later he came upon Oddie's Trains, tucked away but probably well-known to a small and monomaniacal clique of customers. Charlie had to admit he was enchanted by the display in the window of the Rocket, the Royal Scot, and the latest train in the Virgin squad of which so much was promised. He was a little boy again by the time Mike spotted him from inside and came out to drag him over the threshold.

'Come in and have a look at something. I've chosen the most suitable train for the four-year-old daughter of a rising police-man, and it's a present, so you can't quarrel with my choice. It's good to see you, Charlie. No starry-eyed little customers at the moment, so it's ideal. Why don't you sit down and tell me what you want done.'

When they were settled down around the counter, surrounded by steam and diesel engines drawing passenger or freight stock of ancient and modern design, Charlie got straight to business.

'You guessed it was about Coggenhoe's death. I don't like calling him Dad, and it's something I never did to his face. I'll tell you right away that the connection with what I want you to get on to is almost non-existent, but even so putting you on to this chap is a little bit distasteful. The man has become a friend since we moved to Slepton Edge; in fact he and his wife are our best friends there. His name is Chris Carlson, he's early to mid-thirties, wife expecting. He's a retired medical consultant, or perhaps one just taking time out. He's dabbling in local politics, taking a totally independent line, and not doing too badly. Makes a sort of living by painting local scenes – solid middle-of-the-road kinds of pictures, quite attractive.'

'I think I registered him when he did quite well in the election for mayor earlier this year. He didn't sound a middle-of-the-road kind of person.'

'He's not. If he's anything it's a maverick. The other thing that marks him off is that he's become a sort of Father Confessor figure for Slepton – or an agony aunt if you prefer. He's so likeable and sympathetic that people come to him with their problems.'

'Is that what Rupert Coggenhoe did?'

'No – not at all. Chris did try to offer him advice – not his usual practice, but he knew we were worried about him – but he was slapped down.'

'What was the advice about?'

Charlie shifted uneasily in his chair.

'A relationship that seemed to be developing with a young girl – a fifteen-year-old one. I stress "seemed", because Felicity and I don't think it was a sexual thing at all, more a master-and-willing-slave one. Something of the sort had happened in Coombe

Barton, where he used to live. He'd been forced to decamp and come north.'

'To live with you? How did you get on?'

'Edgily. No explosions, no warmth. But he was near, not with.'

'And it's this Chris Carlson you want investigated?'

'Yes, and I feel rotten about it.'

'Save me your moral agonies. What is it you want to know?'

'Parents, birth, education, medical career, why that career was given up. And anything you can pick up by the wayside.'

'Shouldn't be too much trouble. I don't think we'll get much on the usual electronic information purveyors–'

'No, I thought not.'

'–but once I get the place and date of birth it should be fairly plain sailing. There are medical directories and so on, and they're fairly up to date, though of course we won't find any scandals there, any more than we would in Crockfords.'

'If you want scandals about vicars you go to the local newspapers and the *News of the World*. Both of these are pretty good on scandals involving professional men or women in general.'

'They are. So leave it with me. I'm shutting for lunch now. Come with me and we'll take Margaret out for a pub lunch.'

The lunch was hasty but pleasant, and

Oddie's wife was delighted to renew her acquaintanceship with Charlie. She asked who the mystery man was that her husband was to look into.

'A friend,' said Charlie. 'And a friend with only the slightest connection with Rupert Coggenhoe. He tried to warn him – usually silly, and with Rupert predictably useless. He was bound to just continue on his way.'

'And who is this friend?'

'He was a hospital consultant. He quit the job because of disgust at the way the Health Service is being run – becoming a sausage machine, run by management men obsessed with waiting times and patient turnover: heartless, soulless, that's what he thinks. I've every reason to believe those really were his feelings. But were they the reason he quit? Why is he so cagey about everything that he did or that happened to him before he came to Slepton Edge? I'd like to clear up that definite mystery and see if there is any possible connection with how Felicity's father met his death.' It sounded feeble, but he knew that both Mike and Margaret trusted his judgment. The question wouldn't go away as he worked through the afternoon at Millgarth Police Headquarters in Leeds. It was pure coincidence that on his way home he had to call in at the General Infirmary to collect a confidential report on a uniformed constable who was showing signs of breaking up. He was just taking charge of the grey folder in the foyer when he saw Alison Carlson coming slowly and heavily down the stairs. Her face looked frazzled and exhausted.

'Hi, Alison. Have you got the car or do you want a lift home?'

She smiled at him warmly.

'What I want more than anything is a cup of coffee. No – Chris has got the car. The campaign comes first.'

'We'll take the long way home, then. I know of a nice little coffee place in Horsforth. You look as if you could do with it.'

She let him take her arm and lead her out into the street. 'I *ought* to be over the moon,' she said as Charlie eased her into the car. 'I've been given a clean bill of health, the pregnancy is proceeding on course without any problems beyond the normal ones – I should be dancing. It's all the waiting and waiting, the being passed from doctor to nurse to consultant like a parcel in a children's game. You lose sight of the fact that what you're going through is a perfectly normal process, in spite of the fact that you're surrounded by others in the same boat.'

'Felicity feels a bit like that, though it's much easier the second time around. There's one consolation: you can tell Chris all about it and it'll be grist to his mill.'

But he was conscious that as he spoke

Alison was nodding off to sleep. He drove in silence through Kirkstall and out to Horsforth, stopped at the Coffee Bean, and got a cup of coffee into her before they really started talking again over the second cup.

'That's better!' said Alison. '*Now* I feel human, not some sort of specimen for analysis. It's so easy, when you're going through the mill of the Infirmary, to think: this isn't worth it. Not worth all this fuss. But of course it is.'

'You've been waiting a long time for it.'

'For a baby? Yes, we have. Though actually if it had been an intentional wait it wouldn't have been a long time in present-day terms. I just look around me in the Infirmary to see a host of women in their late thirties who I know are having their first babies. But we did want one earlier.'

Charlie nodded.

'Chris mentioned this the first time we met, in the square at Slepton. We talked about it, and he put your success down to the fact that he had packed in his job and was living a life with all the bad pressures removed.'

'I think he's right,' said Alison smiling. 'It worked anyway. But I think that even if he went back to hospital work now, the pressures would be less, once we've actually got a child.'

'Is that what you want? Him going back to

hospital work?'

She frowned.

'Well, in some respects it's the last thing I want. What could be better than the life we have now? But thinking less selfishly, it does seem an awful *waste* – of his training, expertise, genuine interest in what he was doing, and helping people in concrete ways. Part of me hopes that this mayor business, much more serious than last time, will be the catalyst to sending him back to medicine.'

'Why should it be?'

'Why shouldn't it? After all, he won't get in, will he? Independents don't in British elections. And he'll have a serious, stimulating, taxing few weeks and will – I *know* – come through it unscathed, still able to enjoy life. So it could show him that he could go back to some kind of medical practice and not wear himself down emotionally to a wet rag. And not just emotionally – physically too. He's naturally resilient, and this could show him he could do a demanding job and survive.'

'Hmmm,' said Charlie. 'I think you're out of date about Independents. Think of that man who became an MP by campaigning on the one point of the closure of the local hospital. People are pretty disillusioned about politicians at the moment, and Chris's campaign – centering on the Health Service but broadening out from that – could be just what the average Halifax elector wants.'

She raised her eyebrows.

'Well, I rather hope not. And I'm being unselfish not selfish when I say that. I hope he does well, but not that well. You think he's started the campaign too early, don't you?'

'I do rather. But what do I know?'

'Intelligent observer. Someone who watches and listens as part of his daily work. Chris should have listened to you.'

'I was just reacting along the lines of the general feeling that when there's a death you pause, take a few breaths, reflect a bit, before you get back to the real world and start replacing the dead person. Everyone believes that apart from journalists.'

'You make clear what you don't like, don't you, Charlie?'

'Only when I'm off-duty. It doesn't do to be anything but neutral when you're questioning suspects.'

'So you're off-duty, are you, when you show that you're disillusioned with Chris?'

'I don't show that I'm disillusioned with Chris, because I'm not.'

'Chris thinks you are.'

'Then Chris expects too much uncritical adulation.'

'There you are! You wouldn't have thought that a few weeks ago.'

'It's just that over time one sees around a

subject, sees it or him from all angles. Take these "personal problem" programmes on television: do they do anything but harm by parading exhibitionists before a mass audience to pour out what passes for their souls? OK, that's different to what Chris does, but he does give rise to a notion that he can *solve* problems, rather than just help by listening to them. I have this feeling that the person who has the problem needs to look into himself and solve it.'

'You're an old-fashioned non-conformist type.'

'Maybe,' said Charlie, getting up from their table. 'I think my attitude comes from my mother. She's an expert in creating problems and then solving them. As I was growing up that usually meant turfing out unsatisfactory men... Two – no four – cappuccinos, please.'

The girl behind the cash desk was looking at him with calf eyes.

'Hello Mr Peace,' she said, talking through her nose. 'I met you when you came to arrest my brother.' She handed him his change and he dropped a coin into the saucer on the table. 'You did it ever so nicely.'

'Well,' said Charlie as they went out into the street, 'she's got an original line in chat-up patter, but I don't care for the accent.'

'I hated Midlands accents when I first heard them, but it was only a matter of months before I didn't notice them at all.'

They drove across the waste land that was Keighley Moor, then on the steep road to Halifax. For the first miles Alison was silent, but then she came out with what was on her mind.

'Have you read today's papers?'

'Not yet. Why?'

'Review of *The Wild Duck*. The two I read while I was waiting in Leeds Infirmary were full of praise for Desmond Pinkhurst's performance. "Frail and infinitely touching" was one. "Rare moments of feeling come from Desmond Pinkhurst's funny and clever portrayal of Old Ekdal".'

'Good. I'm happy for him. He'll be enormously chuffed.'

'He will. And it will give him the confidence to take on other things if they get offered.'

'Best not take on King Lear if that's offered,' said Charlie. 'I suspect he could do the pathos but not the grandeur.'

'Maybe. But I'm just trying to say that Chris can do good, and quite often he does.'

'I'm sure he does.'

'He's a *good* man, Charlie. I'm not just talking as a wife. I love Chris, but I also like him. Often the two don't go together. And I like him because he's warm and caring and wants to help people. That's why he went into medicine. Probably if he'd just consulted his own inclinations he would have gone to Art

School. But he needed to do good and to see it working. And because he couldn't give less than all of himself he hated all the conveyor-belt diagnosis and treatment that he was forced to provide as a consultant. But one day he'll go back to it, maybe as a GP, maybe in the Third World – whatever. We take so many doctors from poor countries that can't afford to lose them that I can see him wanting to go there and in a tiny way redress the balance. You may be sceptical, even cynical – I expect that goes with your job. But you'll see: there's a practical, down-to-earth side to Chris's character, and it'll be put to good use before long.'

Charlie left a pause, then said: 'I'm sure you're right. You know him best.'

Soon they were driving up one of Halifax's daunting hills towards Westowram. When they got to the Carlsons', an imposing stone house, set back from the road, Chris was loading posters and improvised banners into the back of his car.

'Hi Charlie! Picking up other people's wives now, are you? I'm just taking these to headquarters, love, and then I'll be back to hear about your day. I'll cook dinner – or get a takeaway if we've got nothing in.'

Charlie watched Alison kiss her husband, thinking there was an element of a mother kissing a beloved child. Then he drove the two-minute route to home.

While Felicity, with help from Carola, made the evening meal he thought over the last hour, and what it meant. He had purposely not asked Alison any questions. It would have been so easy to say 'Where was he working as a consultant?' at various points in the conversation, but he had held back. With most other people (not just suspects) such questions would have been perfectly natural, but now he realised both Chris and Alison did not want to talk about their past, and the questions might have resulted in an embarrassing blackout curtain descending that would ruin their relationship. And that would have been disastrous at any time, but particularly now. During the whole conversation Alison had not given the tiniest indication of where they originated and where they had worked. Only the remark about the Midlands accent of the girl on the till, made when she was off her guard, had given any indication at all, and that could have referred to a move her family had made in her childhood. Such secretiveness in a couple who were much occupied with the doings of other people was surely unnatural.

And yet, for all that, he was inclined to accept Alison's assurances that Chris was what he had first seemed when they had met in the village square: warm, intensely alive, genuinely more interested in everybody else rather than himself. All the things about Chris that had begun to seem self-promotional were also explicable as a result of this strong sense of good will for others and their happiness.

Many of his ideas and actions could be naive and mistaken. The mayoral ambitions would surely turn out to be a delusion: if he won the contest to be mayor of Halifax he would find himself impotent to bring in any changes. He would be no more than a figure-head, stymied at every turn by the party politics of the Council members. When all was said and done, Chris was trying to bring about a change of heart – something miles away from the ambitions and mendacities of party politics in this or any other democratic society. What good could an individual do, even at a local level, to change people's psyches, elevate their hopes and ambitions? He could not avoid a thought that echoed one of Alison's: that for Chris the physician there was a future of undoubted usefulness; but for Chris the agony uncle only one of frustration and failure.

'She mentioned the Midlands,' he said as he wound up his account of the conversation with Alison to Felicity, over their pork chops. 'The accent, and how horrible it sounds at first hearing. It didn't sound as if the experience she had of it was when she was a child. I'm going to tell Mike Oddie to concentrate his attention on the Midlands.'

13

Trouble Way Back

It was nearly a week later – a week in which Charlie had been busy with yet another demanding case involving municipal corruption in Bradford – that he and Felicity sat in the house that was gradually becoming 'their' house, and she watched as he crumbled toast and toyed uninterestedly with the scrambled egg.

'You're bored and frustrated, aren't you?' she asked.

'Yes. I won't ask how you know. There are probably fifty different indicators that give me away.'

'There are. And you're frustrated because you've been stymied in your urge to investigate Dad's death.'

'Of course.'

'Which police regulations, quite rightly as you keep saying, stop you doing.'

'Yes, quite rightly. It would be ridiculous otherwise. But that doesn't stop me wanting to.'

'You sound rather like a spoilt child. But since neither you nor I was that, I'll treat it as an automatic reaction to a murder on your own doorstep. What you want to do, I take it, is to go round and interview a few suspects, possible witnesses, and so on?'

'If there'd been any possible witnesses in the quarry they'd surely have come forward by now. The quarry in late afternoon on a Sunday in December isn't likely to attract crowds.'

'A point worth considering. Why was Dad there?'

'Yes, true. Of course the person I would really like to have across the table in an interview room is my very self-confident acquaintance Anne Michaels.'

'I bet,' said Felicity. 'I presume self-confidence is a quality almost always fatal in a witness.'

'Never say always, but usually. But there's no question of talking to her because if Ben Costello got on to it – and he quite likely would, because Anne Michaels would probably talk, even boast about it, to her little circle of admirers – he would make sure the powers that be in the West Yorkshire Police came down like a ton of bricks on my head. So there's a big No Entry sign up, as far as she's concerned.'

'And we have no one else who might be second-best to talk to. Anne seems to have acted on her own in her machinations with Dad.'

Charlie was spreading marmalade on cold toast when an idea seemed to strike both of them simultaneously.

'There is–'

They looked at each other.

'Did you transmit that idea to me, or me to you?' asked Felicity.

'Doesn't matter. "With all my worldly goods" and so on. Is it the same idea? *Who* is there?'

'I don't know her name. The other leader of the children's gang.'

'*Yes,*' agreed Charlie enthusiastically. 'And talking to her would be a lot easier than talking to Anne Michaels. Ben Costello may very well not be on to her, may not even know that there were two leaders of the gang. Come to that, he may not be interested in the gang at all. The interest he must have – or *ought* to have – in Anne Michaels springs from her connection with your father.'

'How do we find out her name?'

Charlie pondered.

'Any of the children could tell us. Then talk immediately, so that wouldn't do. What about a parent? Would you trust Mrs Postgate to keep quiet if you sounded her out?'

'The mother, yes. Not the daughter.'

'Could you get on the phone to her, try to see if she knows anything. If she's got a chatter-box of a child it's quite likely that she's been told something, or has overheard something, since you were there.'

'I'll talk to her today, or tomorrow if I'm too busy at work. I need to catch her alone at home, I think. Right. I'm off to Leeds and teaching–'

But they were interrupted by the thump of post falling down to the doormat.

'Another rejection!' said Felicity. Charlie went to fetch it, and came back with a miscellaneous jumble of stuff.

'Crapmail, crapmail, crapmail,' he said, throwing one after another – appeals to change their insurance cover, their gas suppliers, and their sartorial tastes – into the wastepaper basket.

'This is yours, and this, and this. The package is for me, so it's not a rejection. Hebden Bridge – and it looks like Oddie's handwriting. Well, he's been quick. I'll keep this for tonight, and we–'

But he was interrupted by a great shout from the table. 'It's an acceptance! The novel's accepted! That Dorothea Matlock of Parson and Whitaker – the one who was so nice about *The Pleasures of Luton*. She's accepted it!'

They danced around the table, to the wonderment of Carola, who came in dressed for nursery school. Charlie said Felicity would be a danger to every other road user if she drove herself to Headingley, and they piled into his car, dropped Carola off at school, then drove towards Leeds talking about nothing but the new book, *Old Sores*, the wisdom and perception of Dorothea Matlock, the quiet excellence of the Parson and Whitaker fiction list, and much else. They hadn't been so uncomplicatedly happy since Rupert Coggenhoe had first proposed coming to live in the north.

'So it's the one I haven't read,' said Charlie. 'The one you *refused* to let me read.'

'I didn't let you read it because if I don't adopt your suggestions you're hurt, and if I do I agonise over whether I should have done.'

'Now I *am* hurt. I've made some very good suggestions. You've said so yourself.'

'About two per novel. Actually I'm lying to you. The reason I didn't let you read this one is that you'd identify three of the characters with my father, my mother and myself, and you'd make suggestions to make them more like my father, mother and myself. Whereas to me they are just fictional characters, and I've tried to tear them away from real life.'

'Hmmm. I had a suspicion it was auto-biographical. That probably means that when it's published you'll straight away become favourite candidate for your dad's murder.'

'If he's not caught by then. And if it is murder.'

'You don't really doubt it was a murder,

do you?'

Felicity thought about that.

'Strangely enough, I don't. I'm usually a very logical person, though, and I can't find any logical reason for believing that.'

'Your dad was a murder waiting to happen,' said Charlie. Then he realised with a start that Felicity, when he had first met her, was the obvious choice to do the deed.

It was a hard day for both of them. Felicity wanted to celebrate, then phone her new editor, plan a trip to London to talk things over with her publisher (as she already thought of them) about her next book. Instead she taught. Charlie wanted to read what Mike Oddie had found out. Instead he ploughed through piles of paper evidencing municipal corruption. Felicity came home by train and bus, which enabled her to indulge in further bouts of delighted speculation. What speculation Charlie was able to indulge in as he drove was not at all delightful. He still felt something of a traitor, a worm, over calling in a friend to investigate a friend. As soon as the whole family were home he settled down in his chair to chew over the information that Oddie and several hired helpers had accumulated.

Chris Carlson had been born in 1970 to a Swedish-born industrial manager and his English wife. He was an only child. The family lived at that time in Peterborough, and Chris was sent to a well-thought-of local private school. From there he went to medical school in London, and it was while he was there that his parents were killed in a road accident – his father dying instantly, his mother of her injuries five weeks later. A man was imprisoned for two years for dangerous driving. Chris sold his parents' home for ninety-five thousand pounds, and the estate as a whole amounted to a hundred and thirty thousand pounds. A nice sum for a young man, but not enough to live off (commented Oddie in the margin).

Chris was already engaged to and living at the home of Alison Hedley. For the last two years of his medical course they moved out to a flat in Pimlico, no doubt rejoicing in their new financial independence. Their marriage was a church one, in Chelsea, and on graduation he worked first in a hospital in Newark, then in a general practice in Witham. In 1996 he became consultant in the ear, nose and throat department of the Belchester Royal Hospital in Warwickshire.

Here information became a little more rounded and specific. The hospital had a staff newsletter and its own radio show. Once Chris's career progression had been established by various determined ringers-round and specialists in local newspapers, hired by Oddie, one of the investigators was put on to a man who ran the radio station. He had been happy to talk into a tape recorder, and was very enthusiastic about Chris.

'He was a dream – just the sort of person a hospital radio station needs. He could talk about his own area of specialisation, of course, but he had to be careful – and he always was – about using real-life cases. He could make the generalities interesting though. Best of all was the non-medical stuff. If there was something in the papers, or something on breakfast television that people were getting enthusiastic or steamed up about, he could comment in a sentence or two, and the sentence would be vivid and commonsensical. Politics he took in his stride, and he could now and then be cynical, but he remembered that politicians were human too, so there could be warmth and sympathy in his comments, as well as brickbats.'

Charlie saw very clearly at that point the birth of Chris Carlson, everybody's favourite kind of politician.

'Music? Mostly light classics and modern favourites. Anything from "Bridge Over Troubled Water" to Gilbert and Sullivan and the *Hallelujah Chorus*. I even remember him choosing Kathleen Ferrier singing "What is Life?" – a real old favourite that, from the days of *Housewives' Choice*. You could say he was a housewife's choice himself – and I bet he asked for that because some old biddy in one of the wards had asked him to. All the elderly ladies loved him, and asked for him to be put on more often. As it was I tried to get him on once a week, but that didn't satisfy the demand.'

Oddie's interviewer then asked him about Chris's leaving the hospital, and the man was quite unclear about that.

'That was a real black day for me, when I heard he was going. And it was just days after hearing it that he was gone. He told someone he needed a break from medicine, that the system had him all tensed up, and he needed to do something entirely different...'

He trailed way. The interviewer asked:

'I suppose there were rumours? People are always inclined to look for something discreditable, or something in their private life, when someone suddenly chucks in a good job.'

'Yes... There was talk about a mix-up of X-rays, so that someone was operated on for cancer of the oesophagus when there was no cancer there. No one seemed quite clear as to whether it was the specialist who had mixed things up when he viewed them, or whether the technician had done it when he put them out. There was talk about Chris taking the rap even when it was unclear whether or not it was his fault. The technician was a young man with a family... He later left the hospital,

but that may have been entirely unconnected... Nobody really knew anything.'

'How long ago did this happen?'

'Oh, about three years. Run up to Christmas. I'd say it was probably November
2003.'

And there the tape ended.

There was a note from Oddie in an
envelope stuck to the tape:

*I think this will bear a lot of looking into, if we
can only find a way into the whole business. The
phoners-round have made a lot of contacts
which could lead to others. They've put in a fair
number of (wo)man hours. It's going to cost
you, son.*

Charlie felt oddly moved by that 'son'. It
was true that since his move north Oddie
had been a sort of father to him – better
than some fathers who pressure their sons
into being duplicates of themselves. And
certainly better than Charlie's actual father,
who remained shrouded in mists of mystery
so impenetrable that he suspected his
mother had no memory of him at all.

For both the Peaces the next day was devoted
to business. Felicity went into Halifax to talk
to the solicitor who (she had found in a note
stuck to her father's desk) had acted for
Rupert Coggenhoe since he left the West

Country. Mr Donnithorne of Bottinge and Partners received her courteously, offered enormous sympathy which as usual Felicity did not know how to accept, and then confirmed to her that the bulk of her father's estate was to pass to her – this seemed to be the bungalow plus bank accounts, investments and a pension fund, amounting in all to around two hundred thousand pounds, plus whatever the bungalow fetched. Very nice, especially since it was in addition to the substantial sum invested in their house. There were only two other bequests: one was of twenty thousand pounds to the United Kingdom Independence Party; the other was of ten thousand pounds to Anne Michaels. The solicitor told her that the latter was a codicil which had replaced one of a similar sum to Kylie Catchpole from Coombe Barton. It had been made five days before his death. They agreed that Anne, or the Michaelses, need not be informed of this till the cause of death was established.

But it was the other bequest that, when Felicity left the office and began the walk home, loomed largest, with an almost symbolic importance. She had had no idea that her father felt strongly about Europe, and resented what he saw as their takeover of the United Kingdom, their eating-away at its independence. She had always seen such fears as the preserve of cranks and right-wing fanatics, but had had no reason to lump her father with them. The UKIP set-up was the sort of group that faded even faster than it flourished, and she was willing to bet that in two years' time it would be reduced to an office in a back-room in Budleigh Salterton. This was one of the few interests or opinions that she had ever known her father to hold that was independent of himself and his interests. She wondered whether she should balance the bequest by the gift of a similar sum to the Liberal Democrats, the most pro-Europe of the political parties. Probably she wouldn't get around to it. But there was no denying that the bequest illustrated vividly the great gulf that there was between father and daughter, even though they had been living in the same village for a couple of months.

The bequest to Anne Michaels was less puzzling. Felicity had no doubt about the motive: Anne had been told about it, and it had been designed to attach her still closer to her benefactor, as Rupert probably saw himself. But he was in reality giving her nothing: the bequest was no more than a promissory note, the payment of which was painless because posthumous.

When she got back home she got straight on to Carmel Postgate's mother.

'Mrs Postgate? It's Felicity Peace here – you remember, I came–'

'Oh dear, Mrs Peace. I've been meaning to ring you about what Carmel said. I mean that sort of thing is horrible, and it's not something she's been taught at home. Such a lovely little girl too...'

'Oh don't mention it. It's probably something she's picked up from that little gang.'

'Do you think so? I hadn't thought of that.'

'Well, if you object to newcomers in a village the chances are you will object to immigrants to a country, won't you? Mrs Postgate, are you alone?'

'Alone in the house? Yes, Jim's at work and Carmel's at school.'

'I wanted to ask you something, and I didn't want Carmel to overhear your side of the conversation.'

'Oh? This sounds mysterious.'

'Normally it wouldn't be, but Charlie has to be very careful at the moment. He's naturally very interested in my father's death, but as a policeman he definitely can't be involved.'

'Oh, I see,' said Mrs Postgate, sounding as if she didn't. 'Do you mean that you want what we say to be in confidence? I will say I'm not a talker. Carmel takes after her grandmother, not me. If you say you want me to keep quiet about something, nothing will be said.'

'That is what I want. Now, when I was

round at your house we talked – Carmel and I – about Anne Michaels. There's not much doubt she was the leader of this little group of children.'

'Oh, no. I'm quite sure it was her. Carmel was always talking about her – "Anne this and Anne that", until I could have screamed. She's shut up about her recently, which isn't like Carmel at all, but I'm grateful for it.'

'Interesting. Now, when I saw the group in action there seemed to be two older girls leading it. Is there any other girl who Carmel has been talking about a lot?'

There was a substantial pause.

'I suppose the one she talked about *second most* as you might say was Rachel Pickles. Not all the time, like Anne, but she came into it quite often. And she's a girl of about Anne's age, whereas the other ones she talked about off and on were more Carmel's age – eleven or twelve. Do you know Rachel?'

'Not at all.'

'Only they live somewhere up there near your father. Either Forsythia Avenue or Luddenden Road. They're nice people, the Pickleses. But then the Michaelses are nice too. No side about them, which is more than you can say about Anne. It makes you think. It's worrying.'

Felicity agreed it was worrying. Then she reinforced her plea for confidentiality and rang off. She went straight to the telephone directory and found a Pickles, K and W, at Luddenden Road, number 25.

That afternoon, after she had fetched Carola from the nursery, she left the car in Walsh Street and they went for a walk, Carola wondering aloud why they needed to walk when she'd tired herself out at school (as she always called it). Number 25 was on the corner of Forsythia Street, with a good view up to Rupert Coggenhoe's bungalow. It was a nice area, towards the top of Slepton Edge, with excellent views. Most of the houses in Luddenden Road were early twentieth century, almost all stone, while Forsythia Avenue was brick inter-war semis and bungalows, with some more recent houses at the upper end. Several properties were on the market, because house-buying had peaked and dipped, as it has a habit of doing. Felicity's eyes could dwell on the far end of the street, beyond which could be seen the rough path across scrub that led to the quarry. Along that path Rupert Coggenhoe had presumably begun his walk the Sunday before last. Was it just a walk to brush away the cobwebs, or a walk with a purpose, perhaps a meeting? She turned around quickly and made her way home.

Charlie's first chore of the morning was going to Blackett and Podmore, the estate agents in the centre of Westowram. He and

Felicity had talked it over and decided there was no harm in signalling to young Mr Podmore (the man with whom they'd had dealings in the buying of the two houses) that 23 Forsythia Avenue, a highly desirable bungalow residence, as he doubtless remembered, suitable for a couple unencumbered with family ('That means "Seen the last of the little blood-suckers at last",' said Charlie) was shortly to be coming on the market again.

'We're getting in early,' Charlie had said reluctantly. 'Just the sort of thing I've been criticising Chris for.'

'The situation is quite different,' said Felicity. 'Chris has to think of the look of the thing, since he relies on the reactions of the electorate to anything he does. We don't. In fact, putting the house on the market is a way of saying "Sentiment doesn't come into it where me and my dad are concerned". It's a piece of commendable honesty.'

'Hmmm. Very commendable. And it'll be nice to have a large part of the mortgage on this house paid off, won't it? But I think we'll have to make it unofficial and a bit off-the-record at first. I am a policeman. People don't like us doing slightly dodgy things.'

So Charlie was on his way to signal that the property was shortly to come on to the market, and that it would suit him and Felicity very well if it could be sold without all the vulgar business of misleading ads in the local property supplements or placards placed in the garden.

The door he pushed at Blackett and Podmore's was pulled on the other side by Ben Costello, and he nearly fell on his face.

'Hello, er, Ben,' Charlie said, going back into the street. 'Are you Ben at the moment, or are you Inspector Costello? It's all getting quite confusing.'

'Oh, we're in Civvy Street at the moment, aren't we? I'm Ben and you're Charlie. All palsy-walsy till I call you into the station for a beating up.'

He grinned a steely grin.

'That'll be the day. If you haven't learnt in Halifax that beatings-up are strictly for drunks and down-and-outs "resisting arrest" you really are living in the dark ages of policing... Seriously, any advances on the medical front yet?'

Costello spread out his hands.

'I'll come and talk to Felicity if we get anything definite. At the moment all we have is a light bruise high on the shoulder that could have been caused by "human agency", but equally could be the result of a bump against a rock or shrub on the way down. That's the trouble with this case: it's too indefinite. All the experts hedge their bets. That means that even if it was murder we'd have a hell of a job putting a case together.'

'I see your point. Well, thanks for telling me.'

'Oh, I'm always willing to share information – when I'm talking to someone I can trust. I can trust you, can't I? You have been a good boy, so far as I can tell. That's what I hear.'

'Oh, I'm always a good boy. Ask Felicity.'

'As if she'd know!' said Costello. 'By the way, you're not moving, are you? Not going back to Leeds?'

Charlie looked mystified, and Costello nodded towards the door of Blackett and Podmore.

'Oh no. No question of it. I've never wanted to live close to work. What policeman would? No, I'm just going to make preliminary noises about putting the ancestral bungalow on the market.'

'The Forsythia Avenue one? Well, you're not letting the grass grow under your feet, are you?'

Charlie felt nettled.

'Why should we?'

'Why indeed? And it'll make a hefty dent in the monthly mortgage payments, won't it? I must keep my eye on you and Felicity. If ever I knew a strong motive for murder it's present-day house prices, and the average mortgage!'

And he smiled his choppers-of-steel smile again and strolled off. 'I hate sarky policemen,' thought Charlie. Then he remembered that his reputation was of being precisely that himself. He resolved to keep his sarcasm and cynicism to himself a bit more in the future. This was a resolution forgotten long before he arrived into work in Leeds.

'What gives with your Ben Costello?' he asked Harridance later in the day, on the phone about something else. 'Either he doesn't like me, or aggression is his second name.'

'He prefers women,' said Harridance. 'And there are little ones to prove it. Men bring out the macho in him. Anyway, all you new inspectors have something to prove.'

Only I'm a sight more relaxed about it than that twitchy thug Costello, thought Charlie. I only hope that's being noticed by the powers that be.

14

The Lost Leader

Two days later, on Charlie's day off, he and Felicity were shopping in the Halifax Sainsbury's, resisting Carola's demands for a variety of soft drinks and sweets that would spell rot to her teeth. Somehow it seemed as if sweet things managed to make an appearance everywhere except the meat refrigerator and the household cleansing section. It was when they were about to exhaust the grocery section and enter the 'anything you might conceivably fancy' section that Charlie heard a voice from the make-up aisle.

'It's only two periods, Mel: Geography and French. Anyway, we can bunk off whenever we like. We're privileged.'

He nudged Felicity and they looked up the aisle. Two girls in the uniform of Westowram High were peering at the lipsticks.

'I think–' Charlie began, but he was interrupted by one of the girls saying, 'Come on or the bus will go.' The pair marched out, paying for the lipstick at the check-out till.

'The tall one,' said Charlie. 'Is that her? Should I follow them?'

'Yes, I'm sure it is. I'll follow them. You're too conspicuous, and you've talked to the group... I may be gone some time.'

She near-ran, trying not in her turn to make herself look conspicuous. The girls were a few yards in front of her, going up through the little rock garden beside the RSPCA kennels, from which a great deal of pathetic whining was heard. She slowed down at the top, where the girls waited to cross the road, then she herself crossed at the back of a little knot of people and followed them into the bus station. Then she

239

joined the queue which they had joined, five or six people between them. It was the bus to Bradford. She heard the bright, clear tones of the girl she had picked out as Rachel Pickles ask for 'two concessions, returns, to Bradford,' and asked for a return herself. They were ensconced in the front seat upstairs, on the left of the bus, and were already tearing the lipstick from its plastic container. She sat down two rows behind them, and buried her nose in a copy of *Metro* which had been lying on the seat. She didn't have long to wait before the talk turned from make-up to their own concerns.

Initially they swapped thoughts about where they were going, and that was at full voice. It was no surprise to Felicity to learn that their destination was the Museum of Film and Television. They obviously knew the place thoroughly, but talk soon turned to the cafeteria, and from there to boys. Like adolescents through the ages they had a favourite place where they went to meet the opposite sex, and with them it was the café of the free Museum. Felicity thought Rachel and her friend had chosen well. As the talk began to get more personal they cast a brief look round the top deck of the bus. An old couple was asleep on the double seat on the other side of the aisle, and Felicity was apparently deep in her newspaper. Still, they lowered their voices a little once the topic turned to boys.

'Oh, I hope Darren Fawcett is there today,' said the girl called Mel. (Short for Melanie? Or a nickname based on her fondness for Mel Gibson?) 'He's a dream.'

'He's all right,' said Rachel.

'And he's interested. I know he is. You can always tell.'

'I prefer to play the field, Mel. Why pick on one? I quite like Darren, but I like Pete Morecamb and Jimmy Catchpole too. I don't have to choose, that's how I see it. Choose a best friend, but not a boyfriend – not yet.'

The other girl shrugged.

'Please yourself ... I bet we have a more interesting time than your old mate Anne Michaels has these days. I bet she'd be dead jealous if she knew.'

'Yeah, I bet. 'Specially as her ancient boy-friend is dead... She's getting talked about, you know.'

'Oh, I know. Everybody's whispering. She isn't liked... I don't think his dying was an accident, do you?'

'No, I don't. They say the police don't either.'

'What do they think it was?'

'Well, murder, I guess. More interesting than if he threw himself over.' She grimaced. 'Can you imagine killing yourself by jumping into a quarry?'

'No. Anyway, why would he want to kill himself?'

'Too old to get it up as often as Bitch Annie wanted it?... But I prefer murder. I'm sure it's murder.'

Mel thought for a bit, then preferred to go back in time.

'Why do you think Bitch Annie got all those kids together?'

'Leader. She wanted to be their leader. She's got a thing about having an obedient following. I was second-in-command, but did she insist it was *second!* I got pissed off. I wanted out.'

'She must have done too. Paying you all off like she did.'

Rachel raised her eyebrows.

'I saw through her then. Right scungebag she proved. OK, she could impress those little kids by £2.50 each, but she didn't impress me. You can't get a pint of lager for that in a good bar.'

'She'd got other fish to fry.'

'Oh, she had. I should have known that. All those times we kept watch at my window last summer holidays. She always insisted we sat in the window seat in my bedroom. It's got a marvellous view up Forsythia Avenue and down Luddenden Road. It was like she was training for MI5!'

They both giggled. By now their voices had been lowered to something not much above a whisper.

'Or the CIA. Or Al-Qaeda. What was she interested in, anyway?'

'Everything. Anything that was going on – particularly anything spicy.' She put her head close to Mel's. 'Like one of the empty houses being used for nooky. There was one where the same couple went several times, separately. They must have been at it. Well, you wouldn't go and view it over and over again, would you? And you'd go together, not first the woman and then the man. They were at it.'

'Was she just interested, like anyone might be, or do you think she was planning a bit of blackmail?'

'Oh, blackmail, I'd say. But perhaps she found they couldn't be touched for much, because she lost interest. Then recently it was all this Rupert Coggenhoe chap, all his comings and goings. I couldn't see what the interest was. I thought she'd gone a bit touched.'

'She must have got the idea of being his mistress then.'

Rachel's face twisted into a sneer.

'Doesn't it make you laugh? A teenage slag becoming the mistress of a famous writer?'

'Wouldn't be the first time, I shouldn't think. You saw them meet up, didn't you?'

'Yeah. If you can call it meeting up. We'd developed a rule over the four or five weeks we'd been doing it. If the person we'd been getting at came to the door, we scarpered. Otherwise he could see us and identify us. It was always dark, of course, but there were street lights. And it made it more mysterious and frightening: all that singing and chanting and shouting abuse, and then he or she comes to the door – nothing. Nobody there, and total silence. Like they might think they'd just imagined it. What we all had to do was disappear the moment we saw a shadow behind the glass in the front door, or saw someone getting up in the living room.'

'And you did?'

'Yes, we did. All except one. I was in the garden of the house on the other side of the road. I couldn't believe it. We all ran for our lives and hid, but when we dared peep, there was Anne standing on the doorstep, and the door was opening. Crazy! The last thing she should be doing.'

'What happened?'

'I don't know. If I'd known what was going to happen I would have stayed a bit closer, see if I could hear. But all I saw was them talking for a bit, then Bitch Annie going inside.'

'What did she tell you later?'

'Hardly a thing. She knew I was pissed off about it, but she clammed up. She'd used us – me as well as the kids – and now she wanted to be on her own. The only thing she told me, holding her sides with laughter, was that he thought we were carol singers.'

Mel's mouth fell open.

'You're joking.'

'No, I'm not. He had no ear for music, apparently. Couldn't distinguish one tune from another. I think Anne had got a spiel all ready. You can guess how it would go: she wasn't one of the gang, they were all just kids, but she could get them off his back if he gave her a bit of money to share out. That's what I guess, but when it came to the point she didn't need any spiel. He was friendly and invited her in.'

'Oh yeah. I know that kind of friendly.'

'Well, maybe. She never told me exactly what was going on. She said she was going to help him with his writing. He was just finishing a book about some Duchess or other, but she said his next ought to appeal to younger people, not to a lot of old biddies, and he agreed. He was very enthusiastic about the idea, and said she'd have to help him. Get the dialogue right, and that sort of thing.'

'She could do that.'

'Any of us could. Those in the drama stream, anyway.'

'But you've got to admit Anne is bright.'

'OK, I admit it. Even if she is a skunk.'

There was silence between them for some time, then Melanie said:

'What do you think she was *at*, Raich?'

There was silence again.

'Well, she may have just wanted to sleep with him.'

'Why would she want that, when she's got Rich Newcomb and Bill Westerby and Colin Cantor eager to shack up with her every time she clicks her fingers? Not to mention all the rest over the last year. There's got to be something *as well*.'

'Not necessarily,' said Rachel, who, as well as being bossy, seemed to insist on the last word. 'Maybe she fancied trying an older man. More experienced.'

'Like she'd prefer an old banger to a new Jaguar? More mileage? Not Annie.'

'Well, maybe not, not in itself... But if he got her into bed, or even just pressurised her, she could bleed him for a hefty sum. I mean thousands, rather than a measly amount like what she got from the Nortons.'

'That would make sense,' Mel admitted.

'Annie always has a sharp eye for money. And she also likes having fun with people. I don't mean in bed, I mean watching them squirm, or having people leching after her and kicking them as they pass ... she likes hurting people.'

'She does. Likes having them on a string and then twisting it tight... Do you think she could commit murder?'

This was said in a low whisper that Felicity

could barely hear. Rachel took her time to answer.

'Not herself. Too dangerous. If she was caught it would be too long out of her life. She once told me she intended to be a soap star by eighteen, a film star by twenty-five, and a great actress by thirty. She's got her life all planned out. I just don't see her committing murder herself.'

'What then?... Do you mean she might get someone to do it, organise things so they would, or had to?'

'Something like that. Or be the cause of it – men fighting over her and that kind of thing. Or maybe just do something that happened to lead to murder. Annie always has to be the centre of interest, always be where the action is. I think she's dangerous.'

The bus pulled into Bradford Interchange, and the two girls went clattering down the stairs as if their conversation had been par for the course for two adolescent girls. Felicity thought there was nothing more to be gained from overhearing their conversation with the local Darrens, Petes and Jimmys, or even a Mahmud. She went and bought herself a hot sausage roll, and waited for the next bus home to Halifax.

'Inspector Peace?'

'Yes,' said Charlie. He still liked the sound of it. The phone had been ringing as he entered the house, and he had pushed Carola off to her bedroom to do something with her Play Station.

'My name is Ken Warburton.' Ah, said Charlie silently. 'I'm a teacher at Westowram High.'

'Yes, I've heard of you.'

'You've heard about the children. Ganging up on me. You talked to Harvey Buckworth I'm told.'

'Yes. I was interested in another ganging-up.'

'Or perhaps the same. In the sense of the same personnel... Look, I've talked to Ben Costello, so the police who are doing the investigation of your wife's father's death have all the info I can offer. But I had the feeling that he's already decided that this death was an accident – and he may be right, of course. But I thought he rather brushed aside what I told him about the children.'

'Yes. I can't say anything about that. And of course I can't be involved in any way in the investigation.'

'I do realise that. That's why I'm ringing rather than coming in person. Costello seemed jumpy about his position. But I hope you don't mind: I'd like to tell you what I told the Inspector.'

'I don't mind at all. I was thinking of ringing you.'

'Ah ... I should say before I start that all

the trouble – the persecution I think I'd call it – has died down. Now I just have the normal problems that a secondary school-teacher has.'

'Did it die down about the time that the persecution of the incomers started?'

'I wouldn't know about that. I don't live in Westowram or Slepton. But I think it's quite likely. Getting at a new teacher can be broadened out to include all new faces.'

'Yes, I do think that's likely.'

'I can only go on rumour – rumour at school, rumour going round this area – but from what I hear the same girl was behind both.'

'Anne Michaels?'

'Exactly. A girl of enormous talent, I'm told. And I've seen her rehearsing *The Tempest*. Magic.'

'That's what I thought.'

'Very sad. And it makes you think... But you don't want to hear my thoughts. She was behind it: she wanted to get a little group of drama-stream kids to act out all the stuff they'd picked up from *Unman, Wittering and Zigo*.'

'Was it kids from the drama stream she organised?'

'Well, mainly. I don't teach the older child-ren, because I'm new. She used only the younger children, as I believe she did with the gang which targeted incomers.'

'That's right, she did.'

'She had the glamour of being in the drama stream, you see, and of being a star among stars. All the kids watch television – most of the time, it sometimes seems – and they were fascinated by someone who people said they might see before long in one of the soaps, or in *Casualty* or *The Bill*. So when she fantasised about events in the Giles Cooper play they were rehearsing the kids were fascinated, and when she suggested they had a new teacher they could practise similar threats on, they were all for it.'

'I bet. You don't need to blur the lines between fiction and reality for kids at that age – they're still finding it difficult to separate the two. How do you know all this?'

'Recently one or two of the children began to talk. Not to me, but to one of the other teachers.'

'I see... What did you think at the time? You didn't really think your life was in danger, did you?'

'No... Except perhaps in the darker reaches of the night... But we have a child. She was a baby then. When I looked at that utterly helpless thing–'

'I know, I know,' said Charlie.

'And people never really understand the destructive potential of children, the vicious torments they inflict on each other. People may read a book like *The Lord of the Flies*, but they don't take it seriously. Children take it seriously. And then you, the teacher, suddenly come across children like Anne Michaels. First she organises the children in my class. She gets bored with that. Then she gets together a real little gang to parade around shouting insults and threats at newcomers to the area. That was what she did wasn't it?'

'Yes.'

'Getting the idea from some of the lunatic right political parties. But then maybe she gets bored with that, and goes on to something else. It's possible, isn't it?'

'It's very possible. What sort of thing had you in mind?'

'Blackmail, maybe. She sets up your father-in-law, then blackmails him to secure his silence.'

'Yes, I think that's possible,' said Charlie slowly. 'So are other things. What I do think is that she got bored with having an army of younger kids and was moving into the adult world. But all her activities were of a piece.'

'Sadistic in a subtle way?'

'Yes. And concerned with power. I suppose all sadistic activities are connected with a lust for power. I think that with her the power is the major thing that appeals to her. Watching people squirming.'

After a moment's silence Ken Warburton said: 'I hope what I've told you has been of some help.'

'It has, and I'm grateful. What I'm not sure of is how to connect it to the murder – no, let's say the death – of Rupert Coggenhoe.'

And when he put the phone down he sat meditating on that connection. He was beginning to think he had a picture, had a grasp on what had been going on in Anne Michaels's mind, and on what she had been doing to bring about a desirable conclusion to her plans. But there his picture stopped. When she had begun what should probably be called her relationship with Coggenhoe, possibilities must have been going around in her mind: the sexual one, of course, which was in many ways the simplest, and therefore not necessarily the most appealing one to the girl's sadistic nature. There were other ways in which his father-in-law could easily have been trapped – by his vanity, his unconsciousness of other people's ideas and prejudices, his total egotism – the usual state of many murderers and quite a few murder victims.

Somehow or other Charlie was going to have to step deeper and deeper into the picture of what had gone on in the last days of Rupert Coggenhoe's inglorious existence.

15

Life Stories

It was beginning to look like being quite a night. Like most good parties its origins were obscured in the mists of alcohol. At some point and for some reason several inhabitants of Slepton Edge had decided to go over to the Duke of Kent's in Shelf for a bit of a pre-Christmas piss-up. The Duke's had an enviable reputation for food, so anyone who wanted to combine the piss-up with a nosh-up could easily do so. Then someone remembered that Desmond Pinkhurst would be home that Sunday, so the whole occasion swelled in size and became an impromptu welcome home for Desmond, though *The Wild Duck* was continuing until Christmas, when its strong-minded social vision would be succeeded in Sheffield by *Aladdin, his Cat and the Seven Dwarfs*, a satiric pantomime dreamt up by some bright spark who had failed to sell the idea to the BBC.

So there they all were – half the village, some with children, all with a healthy thirst that gladdened the sight of the landlord.

Charlie, sitting with his pint in a corner with a good view (Felicity was driving – one of the advantages of a pregnant wife in Charlie's opinion), watched and listened and had to restrain himself from saying 'Shh! Go away' when from time to time someone came up to talk to him. The only people lacking were the Carlsons, and Charlie missed them. They were making a joint appearance on local radio, a piece of disguised electioneering. But Charlie doubted anyway if this was the sort of occasion when Chris's agony aunt gifts would have been put to use, except perhaps by the very drunk in the half-hour before closing time.

One voice predominated in the cacophony. Desmond Pinkhurst's voice, being trained to carry, carried.

'The *really* surprising thing is the offers I've been getting! Not a great wave or anything – not like that dreadful far-Eastern tidal wave with the name nobody can remember – but still a definite trickle, one after another, so that one can *choose*, which is a delicious feeling at my age.'

'What do you think you will choose?' asked the voice of Harvey Buckworth.

'Well of course I don't have to choose anything!' Desmond said happily. 'I can return to Slepton and go on just as before. And I shall have a *break*, no doubt about that... But I think I'm most tempted by the thought of Old Gobbo and the Globe.'

'Who in God's name is Old Gobbo?' came the voice of Belle Costello.

'Shakespeare, dear girl. *The Merchant of Venice*. A sheer comedy part, so in some ways a step *backwards* for poor old Desmond. But the thought of performing *at* the Globe, in just the conditions of Shakespeare's time, and so *close* to the audience you can see if they're getting the jokes – so unlike television where I made my name! But there are other possibilities too. Sir Anthony Absolute at Richmond, Captain Shotover at Hull, even King Lear at Colchester. But that offer was Colchester's mistake, and I shan't compound it by taking them up on it. Giggled at by Essex girls. I couldn't bear it.'

'Have there been any television offers?' came the question from the little knot of people around him. Charlie thought he recognised the voice of Anne Michaels.

'Dear lady... Dear young lady, I should say. People always want to know that. There are other means of dramatic expression than that horrible little box. I may sound ungrateful, but think how much attention is paid to those flickering images on the screen – or how little, I should say. Half the nation is slumped before it three-parts asleep. The other half is just waiting to press the zapper to see if the other twenty channels they have on offer will have something more likely to arouse a scintilla of interest in their tiny minds. No, I'm for real people on real seats looking at things happening on a good old stage. Just like they did at the Globe. Why do we always imitate the worst and not the best things in the American Way of Life?'

The little group around him seemed to be shifting away as Desmond gave a battering to the cornerstone of the home and family existence. At least they didn't pretend that they hardly ever watched it. Charlie noted Harvey Buckworth, previously on the edge of the group, now moving forward to have the chance of a word privately with the new Great Man. A minute or two later he pounced, sitting down tentatively beside Desmond.

'I was wondering Mr Pinkhurst – whether you'd – well, I expect you know that we have a drama stream here – at Westowram High, I mean, and I wondered if, one day when you're not too busy–'

For a drama teacher Buckworth had very little facility in special pleading. Desmond Pinkhurst turned to him with a dangerous smile on his face.

'Ah! A *drama* stream. A special course to teach the tiny tots and the teenage aspiring media darlings how to–'

'We don't have any tiny tots.'

'–how to "make it" in the world of soap operas, police dramas, reality TV – what can that mean? – and sitcoms. I speak as one who once sitcommed himself to professional extinction. I must say I fail to see why state education should be laying on special facilities – I presume you are a professional facility? – to prepare children for a life on the fringes of the acting trade. Is that kind? Is that realistic? Ask yourself what happened to the child stars of my youth. What is Hayley Mills doing these days? What became of John Howard Davis? The truth is that grown-up boy stars slide into something called management or do something with a high-falutin' title on the outskirts of the pop industry. And the girls "dwindle" into wives, as dear Millamant describes it in a play you won't know.'

'*The Way of the World*,' said Harvey Buckworth bravely.

'Ah, you do know! Forgive me. But I pose the question: is it kind to prepare children for a career in which there will be very little call for their tiny and specialised talents?'

'You could ask the same about the drama schools.'

'I could indeed. But there they would enjoy high-quality tuition and get career advice from professionals. But let me lay my cards on the table. This is not the reason why I am going to refuse the request that you have not yet made to come and talk to your "stream". I was an actor for thirty years before my fifteen years of sabbatical leave from it. I love the profession, the atmosphere, even some of the people. I would never try to put off budding actors with talent and the necessary survival skills to enter it. I am refusing you because some time ago – last year, I think – I picked up something said by one of your star actresses, the young lady who a few minutes ago was in the group around me here. I picked it up with these ears trained in the distant past to catch the still small voice of the prompter. And what she said to her friend was: "Pinkhurst? Oh, Harvey says he's just a has-been. He says he'd only tell us things that are useless in today's acting market." Now, if you'll excuse me, dear boy, this "has been" will wish the "never was" good evening and goodnight.'

And he got up, looking around, and, perhaps regretting that Chris Carlson was not around to have a really good heart-to-heart with, he rambled over to talk to Ken Warburton and his wife, the victims of the drama group's earlier attentions. Charlie sat for a moment admiring Desmond's style. He wished he could say 'Dear boy' with that wonderful diminishing effect. For the second time in recent weeks he had a tiny twinge of regret that he had not tried for drama school. He told himself sternly that he had opted for real-life drama instead of the manufactured kind. He thought of the grotesque unreality of *The Bill*. But he had to admit that the thought of an audience applauding him would have been a fantastic experience.

Then he heard his wife's voice and he went over to where she was standing. He soon realised that the couple she was talking to were the Michaelses.

'Mrs Peace, I think we owe you an apology,' said Mr Michaels, with a rather uncertain air, not quite knowing how to put what he wanted to say. 'Well, not an apology exactly, but unfortunately we've found that some of the things we said when we talked before are not true, or at least not *quite* true.'

'Oh dear,' said Felicity, with a straight face.

'I mean, we've learnt a lot about Anne since then, not all of it ... what we'd wish to hear, to be perfectly frank. And, looking back, we think you must have known a bit about the things that we've just learnt. You were ... reserved, like, when we talked.'

'I suppose I was. I heard her ... and the little gang of children, not far from where we live, and I followed them.'

'That is what we've discovered,' Mrs Michaels eagerly said. 'Of course she put a stop to it when she became friendly with your poor father, and that's another thing we've got to be grateful for, but it sounds really horrible, what went on with those children, and them quite a bit younger than she was.'

'I think it was horrible.'

'Why didn't the school put a stop to it? They were all children from the Westowram High.'

'I think it was things they were doing at school that led to it.'

'Well, it must have been,' said Mrs Michaels, seizing on it. 'I mean, we're not prejudiced people. Live and let live, that's our motto. Wouldn't it be ridiculous if you couldn't move from town to town just as you pleased? It would be like the old Iron Curtain countries. But now a lot of things fit into place – questions Anne used to ask us – where people came from, and that.'

'Oh yes?'

'Like your husband here, I'm afraid.' Charlie nodded, with an appearance of amiability. 'Whether he came from the West Indies or Africa. I said it was probably Brixton.'

'Well done!' said Charlie. 'You were spot on.'

'Was I?' said Mrs Michaels, reddening with pleasure. 'Was I really? Well, it was just said to shut her up. Likewise when she asked whether Mr – sorry, Inspector – Costello came from Italy. I said all the Costellos I'd ever known or heard of came from Ireland. I must have sensed there was something there, some prejudice she'd picked up at school, and I was trying to say "We're all

British". But now we know that Anne had started to terrorise people who only came from down South! Kids! You can't get inside their minds, can you?'

'I don't think I'd want to,' said Felicity.

'Well no. It was so awful that she'd involved younger kids who wouldn't know any better. I told her she should be ashamed. I blame that drama stream. That horrible play everyone's talking about must have done it. Wouldn't you think that Buckworth man would have had more sense than to pick a play where school kids terrorise a new master? He must have a screw loose.'

'Didn't you see it?'

'Well, we did, of course, Anne being in it. But we didn't understand it. Children murdering their teacher and blackmailing the one who took his place. It was above our heads. It just seemed too fantastic. If only we *had* understood, we could have stopped it then.'

'Had her put back into an ordinary stream?'

'Yes,' said Mr Michaels, with an attempt at macho. 'Not that there's a chance now – not a hope in hell.'

'I don't think there was a chance then,' said Charlie.

'Maybe not. The only real chance was your dad, Mrs Peace. He could have set our Anne's mind on a different track. On to writing, not acting. Oh, we are sorry for his death. So sorry. It was a heart attack, wasn't it?'

'That's one of the possibilities,' said Felicity.

The little knot of people began to split up to get more drinks. Charlie too drifted away. So his father-in-law was mourned by two people, even if neither of them had actually known him. And they mourned him for purely selfish reasons, not to say deluded ones: Rupert Coggenhoe was never likely to lead Anne Michaels along the path of creative writing. It didn't have the possibilities for self-advertisement that acting had, for a start. Charlie knew from the conversation that the Michaelses had been clued up on the children's gang and the reasons behind their choice of victims, but he wasn't clear whether they knew about the persecution of Ken Warburton and their daughter's likely connection with it. Nor did he think that they had guessed that there lay behind Anne's friendship with Rupert something other than admiration for his literary genius. A few minutes later he saw the Michaelses talking to Ken Warburton, apparently without a trace of shame or embarrassment, and this seemed to confirm their ignorance of that strand in Anne's activities. When he got up close to the three he found that the topic of the conversation was the dismal footballing fortunes of Leeds United.

It was while he was fetching himself a second pint that he saw Ben Costello watching him from the other side of the bar. It was a suspicious, keep-off-my-patch sort of gaze. He hailed him cheerily and made a mental note (or rather underlined an earlier one) not to talk to anyone with the slightest connection with the Coggenhoe death. It wasn't easy, but he had a pleasant talk with the vicar, then managed to have a prolonged swill at his beer and an equally spun-out wiping of the foam from his upper lip close to where Harvey Buckworth was talking to Ken Warburton. Neither of them seemed entirely relaxed.

'There's a lot of mutterings about the drama stream at the moment,' Harvey was saying. 'I'm afraid it's going to come up at the end-of-term staff meeting. I hope I'll have your support.'

There was a quaver in his voice, as if he knew he was on a sticky wicket.

'You must be joking,' said Ken Warburton shortly.

Harvey Buckworth spread out his hands theatrically.

'But look – I know you've had a bad experience, and I'm sorry about that. But think of all the wonderful publicity we've had from children being in *Corrie* and *Emmerdale*, and think of some of the public performances we've put on. Magic! They've put the school on the map. Winding up the drama stream would be like cutting off our nose. You must see that.'

'I'm sure you mean well, Harvey. And I know you've done a wonderful job stimulating the talented kids. But so far as I'm concerned you've been a lot less successful in reining in the genies you've released from the bottle.'

'But you can't blame me for–'

'Oh yes I can. For most – almost all – of these kids you've dangled in front of them a fantasy world in which they're going to be fabulously successful and become nationally-recognised faces. And in the process you've split the school in two. One small section that's horribly confident and full of themselves and their own brilliant prospects. And one very large section that is going nowhere and is bitterly resentful. It's not healthy. It's not what I came into education for.'

Charlie raised his eyebrows and moved on. Good for Ken Warburton! Wasn't it Harvey Buckworth who had described him as not the brightest firework in the box? Maybe not, but he sounded like a useful glowing coal in the grate. Harvey was going to learn that.

Charlie came to rest beside Felicity and Belle Costello. There couldn't be anything against him talking to them, could there? The conversation was about women's things – juggling a child and a career, or in Felicity's case two children and two careers. Charlie privately felt that women had it good compared to a policeman trying to work reasonable hours so that he had time to be with his daughter. But he never discussed it in those terms with Felicity.

'I think when Little Foetus is born I'll have to give up my Leeds University teaching,' his wife was saying.

'Do you want to?'

'No, I don't. It's not just the money, though it's a lot more *certain* than money from a mainstream novel. I have no guarantee that they'll want to take any further novels, after all. They'll have an option on the next, which means all power and no commitment. Still, it's really the contact with young people I'll miss.'

'You've got children. You'll have contact with the young.'

'I mean a bit older than four or five. One thing I've been conscious of with this Anne Michaels business is that young people have changed a lot since I was in school.'

'Have they ever! I only hear the gossip – Ben never talks about his work – but it sounds to me as if this drama stuff in the school is producing a breed of teenager in the Westowram area quite out of the ordinary.'

'You're probably right. Do you work? I should know, but I don't.'

'Two days a week at the Citizens Advice Bureau. I love it. Fascinating. But if I was advising you on your problem I'd say what you need is a husband who gives up his demanding – physically and mentally demanding – job for something that brings in enough to live on, and both of you have time to do your own thing, something creative and satisfying. Like Alison and Chris Carlson.'

'Hmm,' said Felicity. 'I doubt Charlie's watercolours would bring in much.'

'You've never seen any of my watercolours,' protested Charlie.

'That's how I know they wouldn't bring in much,' said Felicity.

'I just meant something, anything, he'd enjoy doing. Fitness classes, maybe.'

'I've worked in a gym,' said Charlie. 'Never again. Narcissism in motion.'

'But even if he were as good as Cotman or Turner,' said Felicity, 'I know what you're suggesting wouldn't work. Nothing like that would give Charlie the buzz that police work gives him. I imagine Chris Carlson just meandered into ear, nose and throat work, and can just as well *not* do it. Charlie would be lost.'

'Ben would too. Look at him – he's a fish out of water even at a social event like this.'

Ben was still at the bar, talking to no one

but looking and listening. Charlie understood the instinct.

'He's thinking about a case, or about paperwork, or promotion,' he said.

'Don't I know the problem,' said Felicity. Then she added: 'But he's always got time for Carola.'

'I suppose Ben would, if we had any. There again, perhaps not. He knew we couldn't have children when we married. I'd had a messy miscarriage with my first husband, and any further pregnancies were out. I've always felt a bit guilty about not wanting children more. If I'm so lukewarm about it, why did I get pregnant in the first place?'

'Have you both settled down well in Slepton?'

'Oh yes! I love it here. It's just about the right size for me, and having Halifax near and Leeds not too far off is ideal. Ben would be happy anywhere where he's got a policing job. He stands around glowering and you think he's auditioning for Heathcliff, but he's not unhappy, just thinking about his job.'

'I sometimes think that when Charlie's being sociable that's him doing his job in his way.'

'Don't mind me – dissect me if you want to,' said Charlie.

'So you don't feel you come second to his job?' said Felicity, ignoring her husband.

'I *know* I come second. It doesn't worry me. Liberates me, in a way. Someone asked me the other day if we were thinking of moving, and I got quite wild, thinking he'd applied for a job somewhere else without consulting me. That really would cause World War Three! I don't settle in a new place or new job easily, but I have done here now, and so here I'm staying. But it was all a misunderstanding. They meant were we moving house in Slepton, and I could tell them we aren't.'

'I think we're roughly the same. We all want to jog along pretty much as we are now,' said Felicity. Honesty forced her to add: 'Only my father's death will ease the financial pressures on us – pretty much remove them, in fact.'

'And instead of them we'll have the pressures on you to make your second novel even better than your first,' said Charlie.

Felicity nodded, smiling.

'I regard those as the pleasantest kind of pressures there could be.'

'For *you*. What about the baby who screams because he's unchanged, Carola who's screaming because you won't let her have a puppy, me who is screaming because there's nothing in the fridge to eat when I get home?'

'You all have your different ways of getting your views across, including the baby when he or she comes,' said Felicity. 'Oh, is Desmond going to make a speech?'

It seemed he was. The vicar had just said a few words of introduction without being able to enforce silence, and now Desmond was getting up and enforcing it without doing anything at all except standing there. That was what being a stage actor did for you, thought Charlie.

When all the talking had stopped Desmond began.

'This is quite unexpected, and really quite unnecessary too. But I am delighted, because it gives me a chance to express my thanks for all the friendship and welcome you have given me in Slepton over the years. Why should that be said now? I'm not leaving, am I? Well no, I'm not. Nevertheless it does seem as if I shall only be among you occasionally in the months – maybe years – ahead. You will be surprised to hear (as surprised as my agent was) that offers have been streaming in for me, since my much-agonised-over reappearance on "the boards" as we in the profession say, and I am now choosing among...'

And so he went on. It didn't sound like an extempore speech. Charlie felt pressure building up in his bladder, and since he was in the far reaches of the pub, with many heads and bodies between him and the speaker, he ducked down and slipped out towards the corridor and the Gents. He loved Desmond, but he didn't love Thespian mannerisms and clichés.

When he pushed open the door marked with a figure in trousers (as if that separated the sexes these days!) his first thought was that he had made a mistake. Sitting on the radiator, looking fresh and tempting, was Anne Michaels. The only thing about her that was not inviting was her eyes – steely, dagger-like flashes sent in Charlie's direction.

'Seeing how the other half pees?' he asked politely.

'That's right. You could call it research.'

She looked at him challengingly. Charlie was tempted to go and pee at the urinal. She wouldn't be seeing anything she hadn't already seen a great number of. But he thought it would do no good to his image at Police Headquarters, at least in the upper echelons, if it got out, so he went into a cubicle and shut the door.

'What's wrong? Ashamed of it?' came Anne Michaels voice, the vulgarity of the question contrasting with her already actressy tones.

'Not at all. Quite satisfied, actually,' shouted Charlie back. When the stream lessened and ran out he pulled the flush and went out into the open part of the lavatory.

'So what is this research for?' he asked, running water into the basin.

'A French play – a one-acter. *Le Pissoir*. By

a dramatist you wouldn't have heard of called Ionesco.'

Charlie shook the water from his hands.

'Sounds as if he was born in the United Nations building. He's actually Romanian, I believe, and left the country during the War and became a French citizen. I don't recall a play called *Le Pissoir*, though.'

'Unpublished,' said Anne, quick as a flash. 'An early work.' She blinked with beguiling innocence at him. 'I suppose you've heard of him from your wife. Or from your father-in-law.'

'Don't bother to flutter your eyelids at me, love. No, I don't think Rupert was an expert on Romanian-French dramatists. He regarded anything even vaguely avant-garde as pretentious rubbish. He was not an adventurous writer, as you would have found out if you'd known him for longer.'

'He was going to branch out. Become more up to date.'

'So I heard. Was he taking advice from you?'

'Yes, he was. So you needn't be sarky. It was a two-way process, and he was hearing all about the modern world from me.'

'Local stuff, I suppose?'

'Local's all I can do – *so far*.'

'That's fine,' said Charlie, sitting at his ease on a basin. 'Better not let any of the locals know you've used their stories to wise up poor old Rupert on the modern world. They might not like their private business being trumpeted around to a man who makes his living by stories. Or was that part of the pleasure, landing people in it? Watching them wriggling? Did it ever strike you that that could be dangerous?'

A flicker had crossed her face as soon as he brought up the possibility. It told him all he needed to know, though it was replaced by a sort of come-hither look. Charlie shook his head.

'Don't play those games with me, Anne. I'm just a thick copper, aren't I? Not worth your trouble.' There came a sound of applause from the body of the pub. Desmond's extempore (or previously memorised) speech had come to an end. People would be coming to relieve themselves.

'Well, it's been nice talking to you,' said Charlie, his hand on the doorknob. 'Shall I tell your parents where you are?'

A few seconds after he emerged into the Saloon Bar he saw Anne Michaels follow him out.

In the car going home he and Felicity discussed their evening. 'I think Harvey Buckworth is getting desperate about the future of the drama stream,' Charlie said. 'As desperate as the children in it will be. I suppose in the end there will be some kind of fudge: a statement that drama is still of paramount importance at the school, but children interested in it will no longer be set apart in the divisive way they have been.'

'Probably,' agreed Felicity. 'Do you know, when you use the word "children", I react? I find it difficult to see the ones I know from the stream as children at all. And I don't think using the word "adolescents" would help either.'

'Theme for your next novel: the death of childhood. All-right title, too. But you know, when you talk to Desmond Pinkhurst – infuriatingly mock-modest and showbizzy as he is – he's not a bad advertisement for life on the stage or in the media. At least he is still a person.'

'Oh, I love Desmond, and I'll miss him if he's not around so much... But the *odd* thing was–'

'Belle Costello. Yes.'

'If she was meeting someone in the empty house up Forsythia Avenue, that would explain how the rumour of them moving started.'

'It raises all sorts of possibilities,' said Charlie, speaking as one with an enormous relish for possibilities.

16

Higher Authority

'I've got a job for you, Peace.'

The Chief Superintendent had put his head around the cubicle that served Charlie for an office. He had always been a face in Charlie's professional life, but a remote one. They were not on first name terms. Charlie got up and collected his jacket from the back of his chair.

'Good, sir.'

'I've got a bigwig from another division needs to be driven home.'

'But I'm not–'

A police driver, Charlie had been going to say. But he was interrupted.

'Name of Trench. Superintendent Trench, from Halifax. You go off duty at three, so you needn't come back. Be at the desk in ten minutes, will you?'

'Yes, sir. Thank you, sir.'

Charlie sank back into his chair. His dissatisfaction with the investigation of Rupert Coggenhoe's death must have been noted by his colleagues and reported to the Chief Superintendent. Who had done him a good turn. Very satisfying on all counts.

He had been wavering in his mind between writing Trench a letter detailing his unhappiness with the course the investigation had taken, and giving detailed reasons, and asking for an interview with Trench to do the same. Letters enabled you to master your thought and put an argument in the most cogent and convincing terms. Getting an interview would present all sorts of logistical problems to avoid the wrath of Costello, so he had been veering towards the letter option, which had one great disadvantage: a letter could be chucked straight into the wastepaper basket. Now the decision had been made for him.

He got up again, slipped on his jacket, and went down to the public area of Millgarth station.

As soon as he got there he recognised Superintendent Trench. He was short for a policeman, with an incipient pot. He did not exude energy, but there did seem to be a basic integrity there, which was not something you could take for granted in a top policeman.

'Inspector Peace – I'm grateful to you for doing this.'

'On the contrary – I'm grateful to you, and to Chief Superintendent Collins for suggesting it.'

'I've heard quite a lot about you.'

'From Inspector Costello?'

'Of course. He reports to me on the Coggenhoe case. But several people have mentioned you since you came to live in the area. And Mike Oddie is a good friend... Shall we get going?'

Once in the car, and while Charlie negotiated by fits and starts the fiendish puzzle which is the road system of central Leeds, he began to talk about what they both knew they were there to talk about.

'I was wondering how to approach you, sir. On the Coggenhoe case, of course. My wife and I have, naturally, a special interest in it. And I would intensely dislike having in my background the death of someone closely related to me if it was still possible for people to say it was an unsolved murder – even if they didn't add that there'd been a cover-up.'

'Quite. I'm sure you've made this clear to Ben Costello.'

'I have. And he has made it clear – what I knew very well – that I could have no part in the investigation.'

'But I gather you're not quarrelling with that.'

'Of course not. But inevitably my wife and I have intimate knowledge of the victim – no, let's say the dead man – and the circumstances and lead-up to his death.'

'And have you not been able to go into

these with Ben or anyone else on the investigation?'

'I've talked to Ben, but I think from the start he's been of the opinion that this was an open-and-shut case: an accident.'

Trench raised his eyebrows.

'But that *would* seem to be the obvious conclusion. Though I'm bound to say that the PM doctor discovered no signs of a heart attack, or reasons why he might be expected to have one.'

'We haven't been told about that... Could I tell you how we all ended up in Slepton Edge, my beloved father-in-law and the three (soon to be four) Peaces?'

'Do.'

'We suddenly learnt that my father-in-law was very keen to move up north to be with or near us. Felicity had broken away from her family and communications between us, particularly since her mother's death, had been occasional and cool.'

'Did they object to her marrying you?'

'Yes. They weren't racial objections, by the way. They would have objected to anyone. Even the Archangel Gabriel would have had his credentials gone over with a toothcomb. Felicity was not willing to join the Rupert Coggenhoe fan club, and she was assigned on marriage to outer darkness.'

'I can see problems with that if he came up to live with you.'

'That was never on the cards. We made that clear: near, but not with. We did things in the best way we could think of: we accepted financial help with our mortgage on our house, and we found a bungalow five minutes walk away for him. We'd have liked to be a bit further, but for a time everything seemed to be going smoothly.'

'And then?'

'We were always worried *why* he had come. Why move? And we found out quite soon. There had been trouble at Coombe Barton in Devon, where he lived before, about a young girl. Rumours had spread through the town about the nature of the relationship between them, and the parents stepped in about the amount of time she spent with him. After that he had become the moral leper in the town, and he was desperate to move out. He invented an impatient buyer for his cottage there as a reason to hasten the move.'

'Worrying,' said Trench dryly. 'Was there a history of him and younger women?'

'No. And my wife, who knew him best, thought the relationship was probably not a sexual one: the girl was being groomed as a disciple-cum-slave not as his sex-kitten. For what it's worth I agree. But that view took a bit of a pasting when something of the sort started happening here.'

'Was this the girl called Michaels?'

'Yes. I realise you've heard most of this, sir. I would like you to have it from an insider's point of view.'

'You know the police, Peace: always wanting to hear the same story over again.'

They were driving through Armley and Bramley, and the traffic was thinning out.

'We first heard of Anne Michaels in a quite different context, not my father-in-law at all. She was leading a little group of children who were persecuting newcomers to the village. It wasn't racial (I'm one of the very few black people in Slepton Edge, as I'm sure you know). It was any newcomers, including Britishers from other parts of the country. Some of the chanting and the abuse, which were well-coordinated and somehow *rehearsed*, led me to the drama stream at Westowram High. You'll have read about it.'

'Everyone has,' said Trench sourly. 'Proper little forcing-house for young exhibitionists.'

'Right. But with some real talent as well. Anne Michaels being a case in point. She wasn't only behind the little gang. She organised at school the persecution of a new teacher – getting the younger children to act out a play that the drama stream had performed in public.'

'I knew nothing about that.'

'You can imagine how thrilling they found it.'

'I can,' said Trench grimly.

'So you'll understand how we felt when we realised, the day before he died, that Rupert was well advanced in forming with Anne Michaels a similar relationship to that he'd formed in Coombe Barton.'

Trench thought for a moment.

'I expect you thought the Michaels girl was in it for some kind of mischief.'

'Yes, that's exactly what we thought, and still do. We've recently learnt how the relationship started. The children's group decided to target my father-in-law. He had the usual qualifications as an incomer, and they went about it in their usual way. When he came to the front door the children scattered, as they always did, but Anne remained, and had a brief conversation with Coggenhoe before going into the house. That was the beginning of the thing. You can check this by talking to Rachel Pickles, the deputy-leader of the gang, and now Anne Michaels's ex-friend, and very bitter about it.'

'There's only one thing worse than children, and that's adolescents,' said Trench.

'I shudder to think what my daughter will be like.'

'A fearsome tyrant?'

'None fearsomer. But she'll probably turn out to be a sunny charmer later on. That's children... Of course Felicity and I have talked over what kind of intimacy it was between my father-in-law and Anne. It's safe to say there was no genuine affection on either side. Rupert craved admiration and subservience, Anne Michaels was an accomplished actress with an eye on future fame and everything it brings. Why would a sophisticated teenager pretend to give him that unquestioning adoration that he got from his dead wife, but from no one else?'

'Money, perhaps?'

'Yes, one possibility is blackmail: she intended compromising him in some way, probably sexual, and then bleeding him for all she could get. In a small way blackmail seems to have been one of the motivating forces behind Anne's children's army of per-secutors. But when she went to demand money from the Nortons, a matter I reported to the Halifax force, it was a pathetically small sum, as if she wanted to call a halt to the group's activities by con-vincing them it only brought in peanuts. Of course blackmailing Rupert Coggenhoe could conceivably have brought in a lot more, and all to her. But he wasn't a best-seller by any means, and Anne was smart, so she could have found this out pretty quickly. He had only changed his will recently. I can't see him telling her at once – more likely he'd have held it out as a possibility.'

'So what do you think the motivation was?'

'She had a gift and a taste for creating

mayhem, particularly the sort of mayhem that gave her a sense of power. Power *over* someone. The persecution of Ken Warburton, the young teacher I mentioned, was a case in point. But Rupert was a much less obvious victim.'

'Older, more experienced, more a man of the world?'

'Yes, and with no loved ones to protect. Though with this terrible blindness that robbed him of his judgement. His aim would certainly be to *use* Anne as a sort of slavey – work in the house, garden, errands, shopping. But we still don't think there was any sexual component in the relationship. Anne Michaels was apparently promiscuous with boys of her own age, but this was something else. It was Rupert's profession, his gifts, she decided to use.'

'Writing? Did she become his slavering fan?'

'Not exactly. Rupert said that she was his inspiration. It sounds rather an old-fashioned idea – turn of the century, my wife says. Oscar Wilde could have called Lord Alfred Douglas that, and probably did. Ibsen had a succession of young girls, and even Dickens had one. Rupert was often old-fashioned, sometimes claiming a special, almost sacred position for The Writer. That's not just corny, it's antediluvian (that's my wife speaking through me again).'

'I'm beginning to recognise her voice.'

Charlie gathered his thoughts as they turned off the Bradford road in the direction of Halifax.

'But in the case of Anne,' he began again, 'he seems to have had a quite specific reason for calling her that. She was giving him ideas for books. She thought he should stop writing for "old biddies" as she called them, and aim instead for the younger generation. The idea had the advantage of targeting an audience with what you might call staying power: they have a lot of buying time ahead of them, and the old biddies have little. There was a disadvantage in that Rupert's knowledge of the younger generation was hazy in the extreme, but Anne was to be his link with them, would help him with the dialogue, and above all feed him ideas. Anne was pretty forward for her age, and sexually experienced, as I've said. But I don't think what she was feeding him was stuff about sex among the early teens.'

'What then?'

They were driving through an endless desert of suburban housing, each bearing a deadening kinship with the others. Charlie shifted in his seat.

'There was something else that Anne had already shown an interest in. I've mentioned her then friend, Rachel Pickles. For a time, probably last summer, they were very close, and tended to get together in Rachel's room in the family home. It was on the corner of Luddenden Road and Forsythia Avenue.'

'Near where your father-in-law lived.'

'Yes, but he wasn't the point of interest at that time. There was a house up for sale in Forsythia Avenue. For a time, while it was on the market, it seems to have been a place of rendezvous for two people who used to arrive regularly and separately, both with keys. This was pretty obviously a series of meetings for sex, and the two were obviously not any sort of couple. I would guess that both had a regular partner, and the relationships were pretty stable. This was, apparently, sex on the side.'

'But the knowledge gave Anne the possibility of blackmail, or just the enjoyment of the power it gave her over the pair?'

'Exactly. Now the couple, clearly, could be almost anyone. I think it would be helpful to get Rachel Pickles in and get descriptions from her. I don't think she'd be reluctant. It might be interesting to talk to the only estate agent in Slepton, Blackett and Podmore, though of course the house could have been handled by one of the Halifax firms. It's quite possible someone there made the key available, for some present or future advantage.'

'Very possible. But why should the Halifax police force investigate two consenting adults having a bit of clandestine nooky?'

Still the endless, grim suburbs persisted. Charlie slowed down though. He was getting to the difficult bit, which would take time.

'I think I can answer that, though it is with a hunch, or what you might call an informed guess. The arrangements of this couple don't have the air of high romance: no hazy pink glow to them. Purely an arrangement for sex, then? Or could it be something more: an arrangement to produce a child? You know about the Carlsons, I suppose.'

'The "Me for Mayor" man? Oh yes.'

'Chris and his wife have been wanting a child for a long time. He told me about it on our first meeting. He blamed their failure on the emotional tensions of working in an overstretched hospital – he was a consultant, but threw in his job and moved up here, where he paints and hawks the results around the country. He was quite clear that working in the Health Service had produced tensions that affected him psychologically and physically. One thing he didn't tell me was that, while he was working in Belchester Hospital in Warwickshire, there was a bad mistake made in his department caused by an X-ray mix-up between two patients. He took responsibility for the mistake and resigned – possibly to shield the radiologist, who was a young man with a family.'

'Not one of the bad guys, then?'

'Definitely not. There are no bad guys in this, or only one. Chris attributes his success in getting his wife pregnant to his new relaxation and happiness. But he has actually been living this new life for over two years. I think it's possible that Alison Carlson has gone to someone else to produce the child they both desperately want. She met Ben Costello at self-defence classes, where I imagine he was the instructor. No doubt as a doctor's wife she took care at the very least to find someone in the right blood group. There was no reason to believe any closer checks on paternity would ever be necessary.'

They were beginning the descent into Halifax, the valley which in the old days never saw the sun. Trench was thoughtful, and just said: 'You tell me a good story.'

'Here is a fact,' said Charlie, swallowing. 'There have been rumours in Slepton that Ben and Belle Costello are moving – not moving away, but in the area. My wife assumed this was because Belle had been seen going to or coming away from the house in Forsythia Avenue. I wonder whether it wasn't Ben who was seen.' He shot a glance at Trench, whose face was a total blank. 'The assumption that the couple was moving would be natural... And I've bumped into him coming out of Blackett and Podmore's.'

'Go on. I'm saying nothing, but I'm listening.'

'Ben has worried me a lot recently, from the moment my father-in-law's death became a case. There was a scarcely-disguised hostility, and an over-insistence that I could have nothing to do with the investigation (something I was of course perfectly aware of). But above all there was Costello's insistence right from the start, and before any medical examination had come through, that the most likely explanation for Rupert's death was that it was accidental – maybe a heart attack that led to his fall to the bottom of the quarry.'

'Have you considered whether this isn't, in fact, the obvious conclusion?'

'Yes. I'd even go so far as to agree that it is. But do you remember the time when you were a newly-promoted inspector, sir?'

'Just, young man. Just.'

'Sorry, sir. What was it you most wanted to happen to you?'

'A nice, juicy case. Maybe a murder. Anyway something that would hit the headlines.'

'Exactly: Costello and I are in roughly similar positions, professionally. He is a new inspector, moved to your force as a result of promotion. I've been promoted within my own force. I don't think we, or the young you, sir, are any different from most other

policemen: we have thoughts of further promotion, and therefore of high-profile cases.
High profile means press interest. Here was
a possible murder involving a prolific if not
sensationally successful novelist. Costello
was likely to get no better chance of making
his name in his inspectorship. But what was
his reaction? Not a glimmer of interest in
exploring the possibility of foul play. He
seemed, almost, to be *hoping* for a medical
report that could not distinguish any injury
inflicted by human agency. He has wanted
the whole business shut away and accepted
as accidental.'

'That could just be premature jumping to
conclusions.'

'It could be. I'd just like you to keep in
mind a darker possibility. Costello has got
his way. The matter has been accepted as
almost certainly accidental death, and soon
a coroner's inquest may set the seal on that.
I can only put this to you, as a policeman:
that it is unwise at this stage, and could
result in a murder or manslaughter going
undetected. What we have at the moment
are two apparently unconnected matters: a
policeman who may have engaged in unwise
sexual activities, continuing a pattern he set
in his previous job–'

Trench grunted, and Charlie saw from his
face that his guess had hit the mark. 'Go on,'
Trench said.

'And secondly a young woman who has become close to an ageing author, becoming his "inspiration", and supplying him with suggestions of more up-to-date subject matter.'

'That being a conjecture of yours, of course. But what do you suggest is the connection?'

'There could be all sorts of connections, including one between Costello and Anne Michaels, though he surely wouldn't be so unwise.'

Trench shifted in his seat.

'He was known in his old job as "Warren Beatty" or "the baby-maker".'

'I'd like to suggest another possible link, which could provide a neat pattern, but also a credible one. As I say, I can't see Rupert Coggenhoe jumping at plots centred on early-teenage sex. He would have been inviting ridicule, and ridicule always drove him mad with rage. But Anne had another interest: the meetings in the vacant house. Slepton is a small place. She could very easily, by the time of the mur– death – have found out who the man and the woman were. And she could have learnt very easily that Alison Carlson was pregnant after years of marriage, and she could have made a guess at how.'

'Agreed – provided we are still in the realm of supported conjecture.'

'I think the idea of a novel in which sex takes place purely to produce a child which will reduce tensions in an otherwise happy marriage is one that would have seemed to Rupert a modern situation that he could deal with convincingly. The situation could be developed interestingly in a variety of ways. For Anne the next step would be when to make the people concerned aware that their activities were going to be the subject of a novel. That was when her pleasure began.'

'And began to be dangerous. If I'd been her I'd have approached the woman in the case, not the man.'

'But Anne is only a teenager, and she exudes self-confidence: she felt she could handle the situation, she found having a man at her mercy more piquant than a woman, and she was in charge! She and Coggenhoe had a meeting in the church during the carol service. It was noticed, and she probably wanted it to be noticed. In particular she may have seen Ben Costello's policeman's reaction – watching the scenes, watching people's behaviour, and so on. She may have decided to strike while the iron was hot and talk to Ben at once – after the service, or the next morning. She bearded him when he was on his own. He's a pretty abrasive character, not at all matey, and I think she'd get particular pleasure in telling someone like him that she knew of the assignations with

Alison, knew of the reason behind them, and was collaborating with poor old Rupert on a novel based on the situation.'

'Why should he be concerned?'

'I think you told me that yourself, sir. I'd had a hint earlier from Harridance that Costello is what used to be called a "ladies' man".'

'Good Lord – I'd forgotten that expression. Now we just say he "sleeps around".'

'The message seems to be that Costello was a real sexual predator while he was serving on the Northampton force. Several young Northamptonians owe their existence to him, as you obviously already know. Why that should be in this day and age I don't know, but perhaps they gave him visible proof of virility that his wife can't supply him with. I'm not asking for information you can't give me, sir, but I'd guess that when he got the job here he was given an ultimatum: change your habits or face the sack.'

'There have been too many cases recently of policemen engaged in unsavoury sexual activities,' muttered Trench.

'Too right. So the message was that this would have to stop, and a sharp eye would be kept on him.' There was an almost imperceptible nod from Trench. 'I think Ben's promotion to inspector was important to him, and he was anxious that it should be the beginning of a further steady rise in the hierarchy.'

There was silence in the car. Then Trench said 'Drive round for a bit.'

Charlie took two turns and started away from the centre of Halifax to the heights of Southowram. 'Have you got more? How do you think it happened? Did it just *happen*, or was it brought about?'

'I don't know, sir. I can't see it happening by chance. Costello is a three-times-a-week gym man, I would guess, not a walking one. Perhaps he phoned Rupert and suggested they meet and talk. Perhaps he cruised around the area – it's where he lives – and when he saw Rupert starting out on a walk he left his car and followed, or maybe he went round the quarry the other way. Ironically walking was something Rupert sometimes did when one of his plots needed sorting out.'

'It was sorted out all right,' said Trench grimly.

'Yes. So they met up, and Ben said he'd heard of Rupert's plans for his next novel, and he strongly objected to being used in this way. It would ruin his and a lady's repu-tation in Slepton, and it would harm his career.'

'The argument could have got heated.'

'I think it did, and that was the worst that could happen, because Coggenhoe always reacted to anger and threats with unbearable pomposities. At some point Ben's anger ignited – his fuse is very low-level – and he hit Coggenhoe. He fell over the side and to the bottom of the quarry.'

'And why didn't Ben go down and "find" him?'

'It would have put him in the spotlight. And if he was not dead it would give him a terrible moral dilemma. He thought the best thing to do was to get away fast and wait for the body to be found. In fact the call came quite quickly – the walker who found him had a mobile – and from then on Costello was in the driving seat. All his actions tally well with the conjectures I've just made.'

Trench sat thinking. Then he said: 'You can go back to town now.'

Charlie turned the car again, and went back to headquarters in Halifax.

'I can't say what I shall do,' said Trench gruffly. 'But I can say I shan't forget what you've told me, and what you've conjectured.'

'I don't ask for any more,' said Charlie. 'I think those two girls–'

Trench held up his hand.

'You can fill me in on all sorts of gaps in my knowledge,' he said, 'but for God's sake don't try to teach me my job.'

'Sorry, sir.'

'Here we are. I've enjoyed our talk, in a

sort of way. Now you can sit back and do what you were supposed to do from the start: nothing. Can I rely on you for that?'

'Yes, you can.'

As he drove off Charlie felt mildly snubbed, but also that he had been fairly listened to, and taken seriously. He was conscious that in some respects he had held back, keen – in order to be believed – to give Costello the benefit of the doubt whenever he could. Was it just chance that the probable encounter between Rupert and Costello took place at the top of the steepest side of the quarry? Was it lucky chance that the blow that connected with the victim landed on the part of the body least likely to identify it as the work of a human being rather than rocks and tree-stumps on the way down?

He remembered the last line of one of his favourite films: 'Nobody's perfect'. In police work no case, no outcome of an investigation, was ever perfect, or answered all the questions. He felt convinced that his series of conjectures was as close as he could come to the truth, and also had a chance of being followed up by Superintendent Trench.

But until he knew it was being followed up, the case was not closed.

17

New Beginnings

It was four or five days after he had his talk with Superintendent Trench before Charlie saw the Carlsons again, at least to speak to. He saw Chris now and then, pounding the streets house by house (he typically stuck with old-fashioned methods of campaigning, because they put the emphasis on the candidate meeting the people). Charlie also saw him twice speaking on the village green, with Alison in tow, by now looking very pregnant. Charlie guessed that an obviously pregnant wife was a campaign plus, then kicked himself for his cynicism. So when he, Felicity and Carola dropped in on them the following Sunday it was with little hope of finding Chris at home. But there he was, pondering over an asinine question for *The Times*'s Questions Answered column.

'What is the origin of the term "Raining cats and dogs"?' he mused aloud. 'That might do.'

'Won't someone have asked it before?' said Charlie. 'They seem to have an itch to find an explanation for every common-or-garden expression.'

'Maybe,' said Chris. 'Do you think they have someone who goes through all the columns to avoid repetition?'

'I should think they put them all on a computer,' said Charlie. 'Everything else is.'

'What about "Has anyone ever trained a dog to shut the door behind him?"'

'It sounds ideal,' said Charlie. 'A question no one but an idiot would ask. Why the obsession with dogs and cats?'

'We're thinking of getting one of each for Junior when he comes.'

'Is this jigsaw all right for Carola?' asked Alison. 'I should think it's about her age-group.'

'It'll be ages before the baby can do it,' said Carola with satisfaction.

'I'll go and put some coffee on,' said Alison, making for the kitchen. A glance passed between Charlie and Felicity, though it didn't need to. The purpose of their visit had been well canvassed before they set out. Chris was impervious to the glances that passed, and was crouched over his computer. Eventually he stretched his arms up to the ceiling and got up.

'"Why is a dog's life assumed to be miserable and overworked?"' he said. 'The best I can do on a busy day.'

'We were a bit surprised to see you here,' said Charlie. 'How is the campaign going?'

'Not bad, not bad.' He thought for a moment. 'In fact, rather well, I think. There's lots of time yet. I don't imagine the election will be till early February. Desmond has promised to come and speak as soon as he's free... I got the impression last week that Sunday electioneering was a waste of time – people have other things on their minds, especially at Christmas time. That's the only reason I'm home now.'

He had registered a whiff of disapproval from Westowram people at Sunday being used for electioneering, thought Charlie. His reputation for selflessness and purity of motive was taking a bit of a knock.

'Are you getting lots of helpers?' he asked. Chris brightened at once and grinned in self-satisfaction.

'Oh yes we are! A real little volunteer army. People who say I've helped them, in some cases. Rather gratifying, really. And the indication is that the Labour Party is going to put up yet another party hack. That will be a big plus if they do.'

'You are becoming quite a Machiavellian political animal,' said Charlie.

'Hark at those big words!' said Chris, defensively.

'I married big words,' said Charlie, not bothering to mention his three Advanced levels.

'Well, Little Foetus is going to have an

inheritance of multi-syllabic words from his mother and a thoroughly cynical view of the world from his father,' said Chris.

'I hold with the view that a child's genetic inheritance comes mainly from grand-parents,' said Charlie. Then an awful thought struck him. 'Good God. Is that why Carola is like she is?'

'I wanted to talk to you, away from the men,' said Felicity in the kitchen. 'It's about something rather personal.'

'Oh?' was all Alison said, but her body seemed to stiffen.

'It's about my father's death–'

'How could your father's death be personal to me?'

'It's … just a theory. Charlie thinks there is a connection with Anne Michaels, the girl who organised the children's gang we told you about. It concerns the house in Forsythia Avenue, number 15, that was empty for a long time.'

'This is getting curiouser and curiouser,' said Alison, hiding her face by fetching down a sugar bowl from a shelf.

'This house was used by a man and a woman, arriving separately, presumably for sex. It's possible, no more, that there will be an investigation into those two people.'

'I see.'

'I think I know the motive of one of those

people in having these assignations. I thought it might be advisable to be prepared, and perhaps to make a clean breast of the whole thing before being forced to.'

'Did you?... Oh, I think this coffee's done. Shall we go through? I don't think I want to hear any more.'

She seemed to be trying to bustle cheerily into the living room, but the tension in her body didn't allow her to do it convincingly. She poured, offered cream and sugar round, then sat down while her husband went on talking. The subject was by chance apt.

'The only thing I regret about the mayoral bid is that the last months of pregnancy will be a little bit sidelined – from my point of view, but not from Alison's, of course. I have my image of Son and Heir, and he isn't the sort who will take kindly to being pushed into second place.'

'Have you decided on a name yet?' asked Charlie politely.

'Oh – *nearly* decided, but we don't spell it out, because it seems like tempting fate. It's a sort of tribute to my father – a bit Scandinavian. It's Kristian.'

'Oh, but you'll have two Chris's!' said Felicity.

'His name will be with a K. And probably I will start asking people to call me Christopher. It will give me greater gravitas.'

'Just so long as you don't start wearing a

bowler and carrying an umbrella to work,' said Charlie.

'That's not gravitas, that's a uniform. And a bloody boring one at that... You know, I *think* – no, *hope* – that young Kristian is like his grandfather, my father, and is very responsible and cares for others, helps them, and realises he's not alone in the world but is part of it.'

'You want him to be like you,' said Charlie. 'All fathers do.'

'No, not like me. Not painting on a small canvas but on a big one. Doing good to the whole world. That's what I think a good Christian wants to do, so that's what we're naming him for.'

'You want him to be a super-you though,' persisted Charlie. 'A very sensible hope. Let's pray that's how he turns out.'

'The best thing to hope is that he has a lot of Alison,' said Chris. 'She's the really *practical* dreamer.'

He wasn't looking at her, but was crouched over his coffee cup, gesturing in her direction. It was Felicity, sitting beside her, who saw the tear force itself out of her eye and run slowly down her cheek to her chin.

'What do you think will happen?' Felicity asked Charlie, when they had said their goodbyes, torn Carola from her jigsaw and were strapping themselves into their seats in the car.

'Depends on Trench, and whether my eloquence has persuaded him to do anything. If it hasn't, I suppose Chris and Alison can go along just as they have been doing, and Chris will be happy in a fool's paradise. If Trench has done something–'

He paused.

'Do you think it will destroy the marriage?' Felicity asked.

'I'd be willing to put a small bet on its doing nothing of the sort. I think that after a few days – maybe only a few hours – Chris will accept what she did, accept her motivation, and eventually see the baby, *feel* the baby, as entirely his. He has the sort of sunny nature that can do this, and he'll have what he wants – a child of his own. Who can say the baby won't be that?'

They had come to the bottom end of Luddenden Road. On an impulse Charlie turned, not down the hill towards home, but up the road, and then into Forsythia Avenue. Felicity understood that it was to be a valedictory sight of number twenty-three, from which her father had walked two weeks and more before towards the quarry. It was also a first good sight of the house where Ben and Alison had made love in order to make a child for Chris. As they drove up the tree-lined street Charlie's antennae twitched and his body stiffened.

'Look,' he said.

On either side of the road a woman and a man were obviously going from house to house. Respectably, neutrally dressed, they were doing it methodically but briskly.

'Plain-clothes coppers,' said Charlie. 'I know the breed, from the haircuts to the sensible shoes. Trench has taken the bait. They'll be asking if anyone saw the couple who used number fifteen. Maybe they even have photographs of them.'

They drove past, looking neither left nor right, and then past Rupert Coggenhoe's bungalow, already discreetly on the market. At the top of the road, where the tarmac ran out and the path to the quarry began, Charlie turned the car round. Felicity sat silent, remembering the tear that had meandered down Alison's cheek. She felt glad she didn't have Charlie's job.

The publishers hope that this book has given you enjoyable reading. Large Print Books are especially designed to be as easy to see and hold as possible. If you wish a complete list of our books please ask at your local library or write directly to:

Magna Large Print Books
Magna House, Long Preston,
Skipton, North Yorkshire.
BD23 4ND

This Large Print Book, for people
who cannot read normal print,
is published under the auspices of

THE ULVERSCROFT FOUNDATION

... we hope you have enjoyed this book.
Please think for a moment about those
who have worse eyesight than you ...
and are unable to even read or enjoy
Large Print without great difficulty.

You can help them by sending a
donation, large or small, to:

**The Ulverscroft Foundation,
1, The Green, Bradgate Road,
Anstey, Leicestershire, LE7 7FU,
England.**
or request a copy of our brochure for
more details.

The Foundation will use all donations
to assist those people who are visually
impaired and need special attention
with medical research, diagnosis
and treatment.

Thank you very much for your help.